T0114962

Spared

S. Ndunguru

PUBLISHED BY
Mkuki na Nyota Publishers Ltd.
P. O. Box 4246,
Dar es Salaam, Tanzania
www.mkukinanyota.com

Reprinted 2008, 2011, 2015

Cover design and illustration by Godffrey Semwaiko

ISBN 9987-417-04-3 (10 digits)
ISBN 978-9987-417-04-9 (13 digits)

UNITED REPUBLIC OF TANZANIA

MINISTRY OF EDUCATION AND VOCATIONAL TRAINING

Certificate of Approval

NO. 778

Title of Publication: Spared

Author: S. N. Ndunguru

Publisher: Mkuki na Nyota Publishers Ltd.

ISBN: 9987 417 04 3

This book was approved by EMAC on 8 *(date)* 1 *(month)* 2007 *(year) to be a* Reader *for Form* 3 & 4 *in* ***Secondary Schools*** *in Tanzania as per* 2005 *Syllabus.*

R. A. Mpama
CHAIRPERSON
EMAC

SEAL

Part One

OVERSEAS CONNECTIONS

1

When I entered Tom's office, he had just emptied what must've been the second packet of Sportsman Cigarettes that day, and he was now smoking the last piece. He looked up at me and said, "Hi, Chris," as he stubbed out the cigarette in an ashtray with a couple of vicious jabs.

"Hi, Tom," I reciprocated. "You look moody to-day, what's the matter?"

"These people," he said, pushing aside the file he was working on, "think that because they're Ministers, they've the right to treat everybody like their house boys. Nobody's going to push me round like this."

"What's it Tom?" I asked.

"It's this Minister of yours. He comes to my office and orders me to issue land titles to his friends when he knows quite well that the plots they want are in open spaces on the city master plan!"

"Typical of politicians," I said. "They want to please everybody at any cost even if it means bending the rules."

"Did you once tell me you taught him?" Tom asked.

"Yeah, for three years during his undergraduate course."

"How did you rate him?"

"Not of the Alpha or Beta category by any means. I'd say he used to hover round the C-grade in his major subject which I taught."

"What did he major in?"

"Psychology."

"No wonder he's so callous. Very undiplomatic in dealing with his subordinates. You can't be diplomatic if your grasp of psychology is poor, can you?"

"Of course, not. Forget him for a moment, Tom. I came in response to your call. Sorry, I wasn't in the office when you rang, but my secretary gave me the message, alright."

"I'm glad you came, Chris. I've been thinking about the problem you presented at the last Board Meeting and I think I've found a solution."

"You see, the Prime Minister has directed that our Minister and myself should travel to Stockholm, Sweden, to sign an important Agreement with the Swedish International Development Agency. It has to do with the National Conservation Strategy for Sustainable Development – the NCSSD as we call it, which we want to launch, possibly next year."

"How do I come in?"

"Well, I thought we could enlarge the delegation by including you and perhaps one member of your staff. While in Sweden, you could try to recruit staff for your Department of Environmental Studies, and if possible, also shop around for other assistance. You can take care of your fares and travel allowance, can't you?"

"No problem."

"Good."

Tom Nyirenda was the Permanent Secretary of the Ministry of Lands and Environment, having moved to the Ministry on promotion from the Ministry of Energy and Minerals where he had been Commissioner for Minerals for a number of years, and I was the Principal of the Institute of Land Development, an Institute categorised as an institution of higher learning, and falling under the Ministry of Lands and Environment. According to official nomenclature, the Ministry of Lands and Environment was the Institute's *parent* Ministry.

So, if you like, you could regard Mr. Nyirenda as my boss, and in fact he was, in a way; for as noted above, he was the Permanent Secretary of my Institute's parent Ministry. But more importantly, he was also Chairman of my Institute's Board of Directors.

Now, at numerous meetings, Senior Officers of the so called Parastatal Organisations of which my institute was one, had spoken strongly against Government's practice of appointing Permanent Secretaries as Chairmen of Boards of Parastatals falling under their own Ministries. This practice, as experience showed, not only ensured that government's heavy hand was felt at each parastatal, but it also denied the organisations that measure of independence which is vital for dynamic growth. This practice was particularly reprehensible to academic institutions which are notorious for jealously guarding their academic freedom.

A month earlier I had presented to the Board of the institute a paper in which I had argued convincingly that the Department of Environmental Studies needed strengthening in terms of staffing, equipment, and other inputs; for, since the departure two years ago of Professor Eric Mefert and his team of experts who had been seconded to the Institute by the United Nations Development Programme, the Department of Environmental Studies had been left in very bad shape: no qualified staff, no equipments, and no adequate educational materials. The Permanent Secretary's proposal was, therefore, music in my ears.

"How soon is the trip?" I asked.

"In a month's time. That should give us enough time to do some preparatory work."

"I suppose we'll have to talk to somebody in the Swedish Embassy here first," I surmised.

"Oh, yes. I'll arrange for Mr. Lindquist to come here sometime, and we can talk the matter over with him. He's the First Secretary of the Embassy, and a good friend of mine," the Permanent Secretary said.

"That sounds encouraging," I said.

"I'll let you know when to come and meet Mr. Lindquist. In the meantime, get yourself ready. Prepare a detailed shopping list for your Department, and make sure you have a clear idea of the kinds of people you want to recruit. You know, when you talk with these people, you must show that you know what you're talking about."

"Don't worry about that, Tom. In fact, I've on my desk a fat document detailing our requirements for the Department of Environmental Studies. You see, I had appointed a three men committee to work on it some time ago, under the chairmanship of professor Chambakare. As a matter of fact, a summary of the committee's recommendations was the annexture to the paper I presented at the last Board meeting. Remember?"

"Ah, yes. That'll do for our discussion with Lindquist. This man, Chambakare is quite an asset to the Institute, isn't he?"

"He's a very intelligent and capable man," I said. "If it were not for the bottle that he seems to be hitting rather hard, he would be an excellent chap to have around."

"Oh, so he hits the bottle, doesn't he?"

"Rather hard, I'm afraid; and I fear he is already influencing the younger members of staff at the Institute."

"He is Kondowean, isn't he?"

"Yes."

"Kondoweans are notorious for booze. Have a word with him about it. But we can't afford losing him at this stage."

"Certainly not. In fact I was going to suggest that Chambakare accompanies me on this trip."

"Fine. That'll take him off the bottle for some time at least."

"What makes you think that? Isn't there booze in Sweden?"

"At least he'll behave himself being in a foreign country."

Tom grinned at me as he reached for his third packet of cigarettes in the table drawer. He lit up and said, "Chris, there's more to this trip than the signing of an agreement and the recruitment of your staff."

I looked at him suspiciously and guessed there was something afoot. As I hinted above, you could regard Tom as my boss. But the truth is that our relationship was nothing of the sort. I was older than Tom by four years. We both hailed from the shores of lake Nyasa: He from Mbambabay and I from Liuli, villages which are thirty odd kilometres apart. We both attended St. Francis High School and Makerere University College, where I was one year ahead of him. To cap it all, I was Tom's best man at his wedding, ten years ago. In short, Tom and I were pals of a long standing. There was, however, a tacit agreement between us not to publicise our relationship to all and sundry, knowing that progress within the civil service could be affected if the authorities knew about such relationships.

"What else you're up to, Tom, besides signing your agreement?"

"Some business. Point is, I don't want this man to know."

"Which man?"

"The Minister. That's in fact why I want you to come along with us. To give me some kind of moral cover."

I could not understand what he was saying. But I thought it unwise to start asking questions at this time. As I stood up to go, Tom's telephone began to ring, and as he took the receiver and began to listen, I could see from his contorted face that he did not like what the speaker at the other end of the line was saying.

"The Minister," Tom whispered to me as he showed me the door indicating that I should leave.

* * * * *

I steered my Ford Cortina a few hundred metres down the road and parked it outside the Parliament building. The Speaker's Office was located just behind the Parliament building, and I had no difficulty in finding my way through the maze of corridors in the Speaker's Office, for I had often visited this place to see my nephew Dunstan who was one of the many Assistants at the Speaker's Office.

I entered Dunstan's office and made myself comfortable in a sofa seat. Dunstan poured a cup of black coffee from his battered thermos flask and handed it over to me.

"How's everybody at the institute?" he asked.

"Everybody? I can't say," I replied. "They're probably alright."

"I mean my *ndugu* in your house."

"I see, oh yes, they're alright. Only my grandson Benjamin sprained his ankle playing football at school yesterday. But he went to school this morning."

"At his age we all used to sprain ankles occasionally."

"Tell me, Dunstan, what is the procedure of submitting questions to the Parliament? I mean, when a Member of Parliament wants a certain Ministry to answer his questions, what does he do? Does he write directly to the Minister?"

"Not at all. What he does is simply write his question and submit it to us. In fact the questions come straight to my desk. I get the questions properly typed on official Parliament headed paper and give them official numbers. As you know, some of our Parliamentarians cannot even afford to have their questions typed. They simply scribble them in long hand and we do the rest. After typing the questions we send them to the relevant Ministries, usually by dispatch, to ensure that they reach their required destination."

"Good."

"Why do you ask?"

"I want you to do me a little service. I'll draft a question to be sent to the Minister for Lands and Environment. You do the rest."

"Hey, uncle but you're not an MP!"

"But I've several friends who are MPs."

"I see what you mean. You want to impersonate one of your friends...."

"Exactly. Can I use your phone? Is there a direct line here?"

"Yeah, the black one over there," Dunstan said pointing to one of several telephones he had on his desk. "You see, we have to have direct lines so we can communicate with the MPs in their constituencies."

"Lucky people, you are," I said getting hold of the telephone receiver. I put a long distance call to Liuli, and after a moment's delay the voice of Hon. Shedrick Yalomba, MP for Unyanja in Mbinga District came through.

I briefly explained to him the little mischief I was about to do, and he readily concurred with me. So the question I was going to frame would appear to have been asked by Hon. Shedrick Yalomba.

Hon. Yalomba was one of the most vocal Parliamentarians in Tanzania, even if not the most level headed. He had been a back bencher for one term, and this was his second. Whenever he stood up to speak during Parliamentary debates, the Cabinet Ministers were on their toes. He seemed to delight in harassing the government, sometimes even on non-issues. As a matter of fact, it was because of this constant harassment of the Government that two years later he was elevated to the high office of Deputy Minister for Public Affairs, if for nothing else, but to silence him.

Dunstan gave me a piece of paper and I drafted the question. In the question Hon. Shedrick Yalomba wanted to know if the Government was aware that in certain urban areas some individuals were acquiring plots in areas which are clearly marked open spaces on the Master Plans. He also wanted to know if it wasn't true that the relevant Ministry was actually encouraging this practice by issuing Title Deeds to these individuals.

I left it to Dunstan to frame the question by casting it in proper Parliamentary style. I knew Dunstan was going to do a good job of it.

2

Professor David Chambakare was the Chief Academic Officer at the Institute of Land Development (ILD). He was actually a political refugee in Tanzania, having moved in from Kondowe in the 80s. He and other Kondoweans were part of the diaspora which had resulted from political turmoil at home. To escape the wrath of the President in Kondowe, many intellectuals and professionals had sought political asylum and employment in a number of African countries.

Before his departure from Kondowe, David had been a Professior of Mathematics at the University of Kondowe and also the Chief Ideologue of the proscribed Kondowe Democratic Party. When three years ago, we had advertised the position of Professor of Maths at ILD, David had duly applied for the job and secured it. I had no regrets for having offered him the job; for as chronicled above, he was an extremely capable person, except of course, for his drinking habit which started worrying me now. It was because of his academic seniority and capability that last year I appointed him Chief Academic Officer, using the powers conferred on me by the Institute's constitution. As Chief Academic Officer he was virtually next in command at the Institute, or if you like, the undeclared Deputy Principal.

I called David to my office at 3p.m. the day following my discussion with the Permanent Secretary. As he walked into my office, I could smell the *Konyagi* gin he had taken during the lunch break.

"David," I said as he was sitting down, "I have the greatest confidence in you. Without you this institute would be so much poorer. You see, most of the other members of staff are young and inexperienced. Almost three quarters of them are our own former students at this Institute. We had a vigorous staff training programme, thanks to the assistance we had from UNDP, which enabled us to send our bright graduates abroad for further studies. Most of them have only recently returned to the Institute with their brand new Master degrees. A couple of them are completing their PhDs overseas."

While I was thus lecturing David I noticed that he was starting to doze off. I roused him by shouting at him, "Hey, David are you listening?"

"Yes, Mr. Principal I am listening. What was it that you were saying?"

"How the hell can you say you're listening when you can't remember what I was saying?"

"I'm sorry about that."

"Really, David, what I was going to say, and this is why I called you here, was to ask you to refrain from drinking during working hours. If you go to class now, for instance, all your students will know that you've been drinking. There's no way you can disguise the smell of alcohol."

"But, Mr. Principal, can't I take a tot or two of gin and tonic with my meal during lunch break?"

"That's precisely the point. You don't take a tot or two. You consume a whole bottle of Konyagi at lunch time. So I'm informed."

"Well, I may've done it occasionally. Not always. But now that you say it, I'll try to see if I can keep away from the bottle."

He then subjected me to a long harangue of how he came to acquire this bad drinking habit. He talked about the political dangers he had gone through: his brief spell in prison and his subsequent daring escape from it; how he lost his job at the University of Kondowe, and how he lost his wife, not through death, but through his wife eloping with one of the top officials of the ruling Party – Kondowe People's Party (KPP). When he reminisced on this last point, he reached for his handkerchief and wiped away a tear. He concluded, "Mr. Principal, having been forced into bachelorhood, and having lost my job, I became a frustrated, embittered man. As a matter of fact, at times suicidal thoughts assailed my mind. After my escape from prison I was holed up in a friend's home in Lundo. Now my friend, in very good faith, thought he was doing me a good turn by ensuring that there was always a good supply of drinks in the house for me. As he used to say,

'These drinks will keep your spirits up'. So I took to drinking in order to drown my worries and frustrations."

I sympathized with him. However, I added, "What displeases me most is the bad influence you're exerting on these young chaps. I'm told, each evening about half of our academic staff are drunk! Don't misunderstand me, David. I'm not saying that as from to-day you should become a teetotaler. I'm not a teetotaler myself. It's moderation that I'm urging. By the way, even our Board Chairman is aware of your drinking habit. He alluded to it the other day when I met him."

"What did he say?"

"Well," I answered, "he simply asked me if I knew that you are in the habit of hitting the bottle rather hard, and I pretended not to know anything about it."

"I'm glad you did that. It'd be terrible for me to lose my job because of booze."

"You'd better be a little wiser on this matter. Now let's talk about something more interesting."

David leaned on my desk and eagerly waited for what I had to say.

"The Principal Secretary has suggested that I and a member of my staff accompany him on a trip to Sweden next month. I thought I'd ask you to come along with me."

"I've some friends there. Maybe I can meet a few of them," David said.

"That'll depend upon the schedule of engagements," I said. "You see, the Minister himself is leading the delegation."

"Oh, the Minister!"

"Yes, he and the Permanent Secretary will be having top level discussions with SIDA officials on the launching of the NCSSD, while the two of us will be recruiting staff for our Department of Environmental Studies, and soliciting other assistance."

"You say they'll be discussing with SIDA about the launching of what?"

"The NCSSD."

"What's that?"

"Oh, it's the National Conservation Strategy for Sustainable Development."

"And what does that mean?"

"Well, I suppose it involves drawing up some kind of long term National Plan showing how the Natural Resources are to be conserved for economic development."

I then briefed him on the planned meeting with Mr. Lindquist during which the details of our visit to Sweden would be worked out, and asked him to revisit our Request Document, and also prepare a questionnaire which we would use during staff recruitment interviews.

"David," I said at the end, "while we're in the company of these two people, please show them that you are not an indisciplined boozer. You may rest assured that they will be watching you."

"Be assured, Mr. Principal, I'll behave myself," he said.

David walked out of my office feeling elated, and I had a feeling that mention of Sweden had aroused in him feelings of joy and hope.

* * * * *

Paul Lindquist had worked as First Secretary of the Swedish Embassy in Dar es Salaam for two years. This was his third and last year in Tanzania, for, according to the Swedish foreign policy, diplomats were not supposed to remain in the same foreign country for more that three years. A tall slender and handsome looking man of forty years, Mr. Lindquist had made many friends in Tanzania during his two year sojourn. There was not a national park in Tanzania he had not visited, often accompanied by high ranking Government officials like Tom Nyirenda.

When Tom's secretary, Dina, announced over the phone that a gentleman by the name of Lindquist had arrived, Tom shot up from his seat and walked to the door. He opened it, and with extended arms ushered in the Swedish diplomat. David and myself spontaneously stood up in deference to the incoming visitor.

After the usual civilities during which Tom introduced us to Mr. Lindquist, we sat down to serious talk. The Permanent Secretary did not say anything about the top level agreement he and the Minister were going to conclude in Stockholm; for, apparently, it had all been tied up. In any case, Chambakare and I had no business nosing round matters of state.

So the talk was focused exclusively on the needs of ILD. I presented to Mr. Lindquist a resume of our problems at ILD and suggested to him the kinds of things we might usefully do while in Sweden. David Chambakare was on hand to supply any missing details in my presentation.

Paul Lindquist was not totally ignorant about our Institute, since a few of our staff members in the Department of Land Survey were Swedes, and Lindquist himself had played a notable role in their recruitment the previous year.

"Well," observed Mr. Lindquist after he had politely listened to us, "I suppose we'll have to follow the normal procedure. The Institute will have to submit its proposals to the parent Ministry, which to us is a sectoral Ministry. The sectoral Ministry will then submit its request to the central Ministry, the Treasury. If the request from the Treasury could reach my desk in the next couple of weeks, we could then include it in the agenda for the next consultation meeting between your Government and my Government."

I glanced at David and was able to read his mind. He did not like this heavy stuff about sectoral Ministries, central Ministries and consultation meetings. But this was 'official' talk, not the kind of inane talk David was used to when carousing in the company of my junior members of staff at ILD. When you seek assistance from donors, you must get acquainted with their kind of language. You must be familiar with phrases like: co-financing and parallel financing, bilateral and multilateral assistance, technical assistance and consultancy services, and so on.

It was the Permanent Secretary who saved the day. He suggested that the problems of ILD be considered from two perspectives: the short and long term perspectives. He assured Mr. Lindquist that as Chairman of the Institute's Board of Directors he knew of the plight of the Institute. He noted that this was September and the next consultation meeting with Nordic countries was due in March the following year. The next intake of students at ILD was in July. So even if the request for staff, equipment and educational materials could be approved at the consultation meeting in March, it would not be possible to have both staff and materials at ILD before July. So, the PS suggested that the Institute should prepare two separate requests: one as a stop-gap request to cover the immediate needs of the Department of Environmental Studies, and the other, the more comprehensive request for staffing, equipment and other educational materials for the Institute as a whole.

After a bit of huggling and making more proposals and counter proposals, Mr. Lindquist agreed to set the matter in motion. He undertook to contact Mr. Erick Betelsen, the Senior Programme Officer at the SIDA Office in Dar es Salaam who would make the necessary arrangements for us.

During the following three weeks David and I had no fewer than six meetings at the SIDA office in Dar es Salaam, and during this period messages were telexed to various destinations in Sweden, including Stockholm and Upsalla University.

3

The Minister for Lands and Environment was Hon. Peter Msokonde. At thirty six, he was the youngest member of the Cabinet, and as noted above, he had been one of my Psychology students during his undergraduate days at the University of Dar es Salaam. But although he had generally been below average in his scholastic achievement at the University, he had nevertheless been a political activist among his fellow students, and his activities had not gone unnoticed by the party bosses. So active had he been in the University wing of the youth league that immediately after graduation he had been appointed to one of the numerous departments at the ruling party headquarters. From humble beginnings he had climbed up the political ladder until finally, he had headed the prestigious department of Mobilization and Propaganda.

During a minor cabinet reshuffle a year ago, His Excellency, the President, had nominated Peter Msokonde a National Member of Parliament and appointed him Minister for Lands and Environment. Such meteoric rise to positions of eminence are not uncommon in Third World countries. All you require is to have your name mentioned at the right time to the right people. But if due regard is not given to such things as age, education and experience, and instead promotions are made on the basis of irrelevant reasons such as 'this is one of us', then one of two things may happen: either the incumbent gets spoiled by being inebriated by his own pomposity, or he breeds resentment among his more deserving subordinates.

Such was the case with Peter Msokonde. He was six years younger than Tom, his Permanent Secretary; ten years younger than myself, his former Professor; and twelve years younger than David Chambakare. Not only that, but Tom and myself were holders of second degrees: he in Economics and I in Education, while David had a Doctorate in Maths. So the trip we were about to make to Sweden was to be led not only by the youngest member of the group, but also by the least qualified academically.

The Hon. Minister invited David and I to his office a few days before departure to tie up some loose ends connected with our impending trip. The Permanent Secretary was also in attendance at the meeting.

The young Minister was sitting behind an immaculately polished executive desk on which were placed two small flags: the National Flag and the Flag of the ruling Party. When he saw me entering, he stood up and started moving to a side conference table.

"Hi, *Mzee, karibu*," he said, showing me to a chair. "You rarely come to my office. It's good to drop in sometimes, even when you've nothing official to discuss. You're my former teacher, so feel free to drop in anytime and give me moral encouragement."

"Oh, that's very kind of you," I said. "But you people are so busy with matters of state, I hate to inflict myself on you unnecessarily."

"Not you. You don't need an appointment to see me. After all that you did for me at the University, how can I dislike seeing you," he said smiling broadly, and obviously recalling the hours I used to spend giving him special tuition. Then he turned to look at Tom and said, "Over to you, Tom. What's it we're discussing?"

Tom distributed to all of us, including the Minister, typed sheets of paper. This was the itinerary of our planned visit to Sweden which had been carefully worked out by the Swedish Embassy and the SIDA Office in Dar es Salaam. It was very detailed. From the day of our arrival in Stockholm to the day of our departure, all our engagements, whether official or simply social, were recorded.

I noticed from the itinerary that except for a few social functions such as receptions at the Tanzania Ambassador's residence, or at the home of the Director General of SIDA, or the reception to be hosted by the Swedish Minister for Lands and Environment, David and I would be on our own, while our Minister and his Permanent Secretary would be on theirs. This was understandable, of course, since David and I had nothing to do with the top level meetings the Minister was going to hold, just as the two government officials had no business meddling directly in the affairs of ILD.

The Minister made one or two minor changes on the time table, and we also made a few changes with regard to our visit to Upsalla University where we had planned to conduct our staff recruitment interviews under the Chairmanship of Professor Finn Samwelson who had once taught at ILD.

We left the Minister's Office and followed Tom into his office at the other end of the corridor. Tom meant to telephone the Swedish Embassy and SIDA informing them about the few changes and additions we had made in the itinerary. He lifted the receiver and listened. It was the Minister speaking. After their brief conversation, Tom rang the Swedish Embassy. Presently Tom's Secretary walked in carrying a blue covered file marked 'Confidential'. She placed it on Tom's desk and said that a messenger had just brought it from the Minister's office. In fact Tom knew that the file was on its way to his office, for that was what the Minister had told him over the phone.

Apparently as soon as we had left Mr. Msokonde's office he had settled down to look at some of the files in the in-tray and had tumbled upon the file which normally contained correspondence from the Speaker's office. He had quickly read Hon. Shedrick Yalomba's question, and it had given him the jitters. He had quickly scribbled a note to his Permanent Secretary instructing him to prepare a reply vehemently denying that his Ministry knew anything mentioned in Shedrick's question.

Tom read the neatly typed question from the Speaker's office and then glanced at the note scribbled by the Minister. He chuckled maliciously, lit his cigarette and said, "He's had it! I warned him several times not to entertain such requests, but he wouldn't listen; and now he wants me to help him tell lies to Parliament! No, not me. He'll have to do it himself."

"What's it, Tom? We can't follow you," I said.

"Oh, it's this man again," Tom said beckoning me to move closer to his desk. "See this!" He showed me the question from the Speaker's Office, making sure David didn't see it. "And now, look at this," he said showing me the note from the Minister.

I chuckled heartily to myself especially when I saw what a splendid job Dunstan had done. The question I had framed had not only been couched in elegant Parliamentary language, but Dunstan had also added part (c) to it which demanded to know who had been allocated plots X, Y, Z in towns B,C,D. These were true examples of plots created out of open spaces and which had been allocated to Mr. Msokonde's friends which I had mentioned to Dunstan. I had acquired this information from Tom, of course.

"Why do you laugh?" Tom asked.

"Because my plan seems to have worked."

"How d'you mean your plan?"

"I wanted to do you a little service, Tom."

"A service?"

"Yes, I meant to scare the wits out of him, so he wouldn't trouble you again."

"You mean you cooked this question, and not Shedrick?"

"Cooked it the same day I left your office, after you'd complained about it".

"How did you do it?"

"Simply colluded with my nephew at the Speaker's office."

"Good heavens, no! You're a clever devil, aren't you? But how about Shedrick, won't he deny ever having asked such a question?"

"Rang him the same afternoon, and got his consent."

"Good! Good! That's really great. From the way he sounded on the phone, he's already scared stiff. I suppose the only thing he can do is meet Shedrick face to face and talk him out of it. Isn't somebody free to withdraw a question already submitted to the Speaker's Office?"

"I suppose it is."

"When is the next Parliament Session?"

"Four months from now, I think."

"Somehow we've to talk Shedrick out of it well before Parliament meets, so he can withdraw the question."

"Don't worry about that. I've already taken care of it. Shedrick is going to withdraw the question at the right time."

"Good."

4

The SAS Boeing 737 touched down at the international airport outside Stockholm at 2 p.m. on Wednesday. To meet us at the airport were Mr. Erick Jacobsson – the Swedish Minister for Lands and Environment, Mr. Larson from SIDA headquarters, and Mr. Lindquist from Dar who had arrived a week ahead of us. There were also Mr. Mhina, the Tanzania Ambassador and another official from the Tanzania Embassy. There was also a young Swedish lady whom I took to be a member of the welcoming party. It appeared that both the Swedish Minister and the SIDA official took this lady to be an employee of the Tanzania embassy or someone who had worked in Tanzania and who had come to greet people she had known in Tanzania.

She was smartly dressed in a light blue two piece suit with a matching hat and silk scarf. She was about twenty-four. She greeted us warmly on the tarmac just as we were about to enter the airport building. She shook hands with Tom and gave him such a smashing smile, I had no doubt, having known Tom all my life, that there was something between these two.

As we started moving into the airport building and nobody seemed to mind what everybody else was doing, I noticed the young lady walking close to Tom and pushing something into his hand, and Tom promptly pocketing it. Presently we were ushered into the VIP lounge. But as there were many other dignitaries entering the VIP lounge at the same time, I momentarily lost sight of the smashing young lady. After we'd settled down to await the protocol officers to sort out our arrival formalities, I noticed to my surprise, that the young lady had disappeared.

It seemed to me that she had come on a mission to pass some kind of information to Tom. But who was she? What was her relationship with Tom, and how did she know about our arrival? I didn't want to embarrass Tom by asking him questions about this woman; at least not now. But I still remembered Tom's hint that there was more to this visit than the signing of an Agreement.

We left the airport in four separate cars. Our Minister and his Permanent Secretary entered Ambassador Mhina's official car on which was hoisted the Tanzania flag; David and I were taken in Mr. Lindquist's car, while the Swedish Minister used his official car bearing the Swedish flag, and Mr. Larson used his own car.

Ambassador Mhina had booked us at Diplomat Hotel, very close to the sea front and within walking distance to the Stockholm opera house, and also not too far from an ancient palace now turned into a museum housing royal crowns and jewellery and used mainly as a tourist attraction.

Minister Peter Msokonde was given Room 305, an executive suite on the third floor of the hotel, while Tom Nyirenda and the two of us got rooms on the second floor. Tom's room was a double bedroom at the end of the corridor, while David and I had ordinary single bed rooms near the opposite end of the corridor.

Business started promptly the following morning after two cars had picked us from the hotel and dropped us at the SIDA headquarters. We parted company in the lobby of the building housing the SIDA offices: the Minister and his Permanent Secretary going one way, and David and I another way. There was thus no way we could know what our colleagues were doing, and they didn't know how we were faring.

We spent the whole of Thursday and Friday discussing the needs of ILD on the basis of the document we had prepared, a copy of which had been sent to SIDA well before our arrival. It was a very fruitful discussion, thanks to the support of Mr. Lindquist who never left us during the discussions.

Concrete decisions were reached on the question of procurement of materials, not only for the department of Environmental Studies, but also for the other departments of ILD. Of course, we followed the suggestion made by the Permanent Secretary in Dar es Salaam, so that the department of Environmental Studies had priority of consideration. Only the question of staff recruitment remained untackled. This was put off until the following week when we would move to Upsalla University and conduct recruitment interviews in the company of Professor Samwelson.

I returned to my room in Diplomat Hotel at 5 0'clock that Friday feeling rather exhausted after a grueling day of discussions at the SIDA headquarters. I removed my jacket, tie and shoes and threw myself into bed.

I must've dozed off for fifteen minutes; for when I was startled by the ringing telephone, I glanced at my watch and realized some fifteen minutes or so had elapsed since I came into the room.

"Hallo," I said, not knowing who was ringing.

"Hallo, Chris, it's Tom speaking. What are you doing right now?"

"Just relaxing."

"Why don't you nip in my room for a chat?"

"Okay, I will be with you in a moment."

I put on my shoes, locked the door and walked along the corridor to Tom's room. When I entered Tom's room I expected to see him alone. I was sure Tom had invited me for a drink, knowing that these VIP rooms often have fully stocked bars. To my surprise, I saw seated on the sofa the mysterious young lady who had come to meet us at the airport on our day of arrival. She was drinking sherry. As soon as she saw me she stood up and gave me the same captivating smile I had seen her give when she greeted Tom at the Airport.

"Meet Linda," Tom said as he introduced her to me. "Linda Wickman, who worked in our Ministry in Dar es Salaam for sometime last year." Turning to me, Tom said, "Linda, this is Chris, the Principal of ILD and an old friend of mine; the one I mentioned to you."

Linda stretched her hand and we shook hands.

"Pleased to meet you, Chris," she said.

"Pleased to meet you, Linda," I echoed.

"I've been to the ILD. I visited it several times when I was in Dar. You had some Swedish teachers there, you remember, and I used to visit them occasionally. It's only that I had no chance of meeting you face to face."

"Wait a moment, wait a moment", I said tapping my head. "Now that you say it, I think we may have met before. Remember the party I hosted at Agip Motel to say farewell to Mr. Lindberg? Weren't you at that party?"

"Of course, I was. I still recall the speech Lindberg made at that party to the effect that he was hoping to return to Tanzania someday, if not to teach at ILD, at least to look for his girl friends!"

We all laughed. Tom poured me a drink and fixed his gaze on me. He said, "Chris, I'm going away with Linda for the weekend. I'll be back Sunday evening. If the Minister inquires about me, tell him a relative of mine working in Lulea took me home for the weekend."

It wasn't for me to start asking questions now, so I simply nodded in agreement, finished my drink, said goodbye to Linda and Tom, and left the room.

David and I had been scheduled to hold interviews at Upsalla University beginning at 11.00 hours the following Monday. An official from SIDA headquarters was to pick us up from Diplomat Hotel immediately after breakfast on Monday and drive us to Upsalla. As I had expected to see Tom at breakfast that Monday morning I had not bothered to ring him in his room to find out if he was back. But at breakfast Tom had not shown up, neither had the Minister. In a way, this was fortunate because I did not like the idea of having to explain Tom's absence to the Minister, in case he had not returned to Stockholm.

The drive to Upsalla was uneventful, although to me, visiting Sweden for the first time, the landscape we passed through was breathtaking in its beauty. Seeing the wooded country side, the well laid out farms, the ubiquitous lakes and the undulating hills which are, in fact, the end moraines left after the great ice age, I was thrilled. In particular I was intrigued to see on both sides of the road, miles and miles of wire fencing. Our driver explained to us that these fences were meant to keep wild animals from crossing the roads thus preventing accidents to the motorists as well as to the animals themselves.

Indeed, looking at the landscape one could not help feeling that to the Swedes nature conservation or environmental protection is not just an empty phrase. It means something; for they do take meticulous care of their environment.

We drove straight to Professor Samwelson's office at the University of Upsalla. Finn Samwelson had short-listed ten applicants for the teaching jobs we had advertised in one of the Swedish papers the previous month. Since we actually needed only six teachers, we had plenty to choose from.

The interviews went smoothly and we were able to pick the six teachers we needed, thanks to the elaborate questionnaire prepared in advance by David Chambakare. It had been agreed that once we had picked the candidates, their names would be submitted to SIDA, and as part of the assistance package to Tanzania SIDA would take care of the candidate's passages to and from Tanzania, and also their salaries during the tour, while ILD would provide them with housing and other local requirements.

Professor Samwelson had arranged for us to do a bit of sight-seeing in and around Upsalla on Tuesday morning. Accordingly, he took us first to the Faculty of Biological Sciences and introduced us to a colleague of his who, the previous year had been awarded an international prize by FAO on his work on plant nutrients. This man had experimented on a number of crops and had established beyond doubt that by feeding the plants with definite amounts of specific nutrients, it was possible to forecast with a high degree of accuracy the amount of yield of a particular crop to be expected from a given acreage of land.

In the laboratory which we were not allowed to enter but simply peer from a large glass pane, we saw plants at various stages of growth, caused by the varying amounts of nutrients used to feed them. Outside the labs we were shown the actual experimental plots in which the scientific techniques were being applied. It was clear to us that with that kind of scientific farming, the day was not far off when Sweden would be able to forecast with accuracy the tonnage of various crops to be harvested each year.

He next took us to Upsalla cathedral, an imposing medieval building of gothic style, which, like St. Peter's basilica in the Vatican, or Westminster Abbey in London, is really a Tomb containing the remains of historic figures. In Upsalla Cathedral for instance, we were shown the Tomb of Saint Eric, patron saint of Sweden. Indeed it was awe inspiring walking among Tombs and works of art in this edifice.

Our sight-seeing that Tuesday morning ended at around 11.00 a.m., and we drove back to Professor Samwelson's office to collect our brief cases, ready for the long drive back to Stockholm. As Samwelson had had no time to read the day's papers that morning since his time had been occupied in showing us around Upsalla, the first thing he did when he got into his office was to glance at the papers his Secretary had placed on the desk. They were all written in Swedish, of course, that's why we had no interest in them.

But Professor Samwelson's eyes rested on a front page heading of one of the papers which he translated to us. It read, "Multi-millionaire's daughter abducted". Finn silently read the article and shook his head saying, "These things are becoming rather common these days. Only a couple of months ago something similar happened in Goteborg in the south-west, and this time it's happened in Lulea in the far north-east."

He translated the article for us and this is what he said, "Linda Wickman, the twenty-four year old daughter of Martin Wickman, the Lulea multi-millionaire, was abducted last Sunday by three hooded men. Abducted with her was an African man who, it appears, had been staying with the Wickmans. A message faxed to Mr. Wickman from the iron mining town of Kiruna in the far North, and signed in Linda's handwriting, says that the two were abducted at gun point as they were strolling in the spacious gardens of Mr. Wickman's castle. After driving the hostages around Lulea for sometime, the African was set free at a lonely spot in the outskirts of Lulea, and the kidnappers drove overnight to Kiruna where they forced Linda to write the message which was later faxed to Mr. Wickman.

"Linda fears that her African companion may have been shot; for when he was being released one of the thugs escorted him outside the van, and Linda heard a gunshot before the thug re-entered the van. But so far no dead body has been found anywhere.

"From Kiruna, the message says, the party continued to Abisko national park close to the Norwegian border. That is where their hide out is, and that is where they are holding Linda Wickman hostage. The kidnappers did not demand ransom money but ten kilograms of solid gold and ten kilograms of rubies.

"Their instructions as to the exchange between the ransom treasure and Linda are as follows: Only one vehicle carrying the ransom treasure will be allowed to enter the gate leading into the national park at 2.p.m next Thursday. The vehicle will be driven half a kilometer into the park to the point where the tarmac road ends. From there on there is only a foot path. The person carrying the ransom treasure will leave his clothes in the vehicle and remain with pants only. He will carry the treasure and walk 100 metres along the footpath to a small igloo like log cabin. These cabins made of logs and plastered with mud inside, were formerly used by the nomadic Lapps when tending their herds of reindeer; but since the creation of the national park, they were largely abandoned while the owners sought pasture elsewhere.

"The person carrying the ransom treasure will leave it in the first cabin on the right hand side of the foot path. He will then continue another 100 metres downhill to another lonely cabin in which Linda Wickman will be found tied to a post. The two will then leave the cabin taking another footpath to their vehicle, and drive off.

"From the time the person carrying the ransom treasure will leave the vehicle, on his arrival, he will be covered by two powerful telescopic rifles whose firing range is greater than one mile, and which in the hands of these sharp shooters can never miss their target. So any attempt at making tricks will result in immediate danger to the courier. But more seriously, as soon as the courier will leave the cabin in which he will have deposited the treasure one of the thugs will enter the cabin to establish the genuineness of the treasure. He will weigh the treasure using a weighing machine hidden in the cabin, and carry out quick experiments to establish the authenticity of the gold and the rubies.

"This man will be in communication with the rest of the gang, for he will be carrying a small walkie-talkie. While the courier will be walking the 100 metres downhill towards his rendezvous with Miss Linda Wickman, the thug in the first cabin will not only have verified the authenticity of the treasure, but he will also have weighed it to ascertain that not an ounce of each mineral is missing. Any shortage in the amount or the discovery of any fake stones will be communicated to his comrades immediately, and the poor courier and Miss Linda will be liquidated without further ado.

"The message said further that while the exchange will be going on, any sign of surveillance by the police, by way of helicopters flying in the area, or vehicular movements being noticed, or the figure of any person other than the courier being noticed, will have the same result – the immediate destruction of Miss Linda Wickman."

As the story unfolded I felt my mouth become dry and my hands begin to shake.

"Professor," I interrupted, "this is a terrible thing. We must return to Stockholm at once; for, I think the African referred to in the article is Tom, our Permanent Secretary."

"What makes you think that?" Finn asked.

"You see, Tom left Stockholm last Friday and said he was going to spend the weekend with Miss Linda Wickman. Actually Linda herself came to collect him from the hotel. Tom didn't tell me exactly where they were going, and I didn't like to poke my nose in his affairs. But what I can tell you quite candidly is that the lady's name was Linda Wickman and that she and Tom appeared to be old acquaintances."

David butted in, "Yes, and Tom wasn't at breakfast yesterday morning. It seems he hadn't returned to Stockholm by yesterday morning."

"Look," said Finn, "why don't we ring your hotel to find out if Tom is back at the hotel or not."

"Good idea," I said. "If the receptionist isn't sure whether Tom is at the hotel or not, let her put me through to room 305 and I'll speak to our Minister if he's there; or I'll leave a message to her."

Finn Samwelson rang Diplomat Hotel and spoke to the receptionist. She replied that the key to Mr. Tom Nyirenda's room was at the reception desk, which meant that Mr. Nyirenda was probably out of the hotel. Next the receptionist rang room 305, and to my delight, Finn passed the telephone receiver to me.

"Hello, Msokonde speaking," said the voice at the other end.

"Nice to hear your voice. This is Chris. I'm speaking from Professor Samwelson's office here in Upsalla. I wanted to find out from you if Tom is at the hotel with you."

"No, not at all. I haven't seen him since Friday. You see, we were scheduled to have a final round of meetings at the SIDA headquarters yesterday and today. But only Ambassador Mhina and myself were present, and nobody knows what's happened to Tom. Of course, we knew you two were in Upsalla and would be returning today. But, Tom, where is he? What's happened to him? I've been ringing his room since yesterday, but there's been no reply. On my way to the meeting this morning I was told by the girl at the reception desk that Tom's room key has been at the counter since Friday."

"Now, look here, Peter", I said, "the reason why I rang you was to ask you if you've heard about the kidnap story that's in one of the Swedish papers today."

"What's it? Has Tom been kidnapped?"

"No, not quite. But it appears that his companion was kidnapped, while Tom was set free."

"His companion?"

"Yes, a lady; so the story goes."

"A lady?"

"Yes."

"Where did it happen, here in Stockholm?"

"No, not in Stockholm. It happened in a town called Lulea, which is in the far North-east."

"How the hell did Tom get to Lulea?"

"You're asking me, how do I know?"

"Really, *Mzee*, we've put ourselves in a mess."

"Oh, not only that, but when you come to think about it, we've also shamed our country, for when the word gets round, everybody will think that our officials are great womanizers."

"Who was the woman, do you know?"

"How should I know? Look here Peter, there is a more disturbing angle to the story. Tom was probably shot after he had been set free. The story goes that the kidnapped woman heard a gunshot outside the van before the terrorist who had escorted Tom out of the van re-entered the van. But no dead body of an African has been found anywhere, yet."

"Good Lord, no! *Mzee*... I'm ringing Ambassador Mhina right away, and am asking him to come and collect me from the hotel. I suggest you drive back to Stockholm at once, and please go straight to the Ambassador's residence. You will meet me there. How long is it going to take you to get here?"

"Approximately two hours. So you should expect us around 2 p.m.

"Right, ho."

5

Martin Wickman was a well known multi-millionaire in Sweden. I learnt later that Mr. Wickman had acquired his wealth from vast mining interests in Africa and South America. In Central Africa he was a senior partner in the giant conglomerate, Anglo-American, dealing with copper mining; and in South Africa he had shares with de Beers Consolidated. Five years ago when the Tanzania Government began to encourage foreign investment in industry, especially by way of the so called joint ventures, Mr. Wickman not only became a major share holder in a number of mining companies in Tanzania, but he also acquired gold and gemstone prospecting rights in vast areas of Southern Tanzania. He thus owned gold mines at Mpepo and Lukalasi in Mbinga district, and ruby mines in Matombo and Mahenge in Morogoro and Ulanga districts.

He acquired these prospecting rights at a time when Tom Nyirenda was the Commissioner for Mines in the Ministry of Energy and Minerals. That's to say, before he was moved on promotion as Permanent Secretary to the Ministry of Lands and Environment. These are facts I had not known while in Tanzania. I knew, of course, that gold and gemstones were being mined in Southern Tanzania, but I had no idea about the ownership of the mines. Now being in possession of these facts, it did not require any extraordinary perspicuity on my part to conclude that when Tom told me in his office in Dar that there was more to this trip to Sweden than the signing of an Agreement concerning the launching of the NCSSD, he knew what he was talking about. Also when I recalled the captivating smile which Wickman's daughter gave Tom at the airport on our arrival, I understood now that it had not been a vain gesture.

But I must crave my reader's pardon, for I'm jumping miles ahead! By the time I was speaking to Minister Peter Msokonde on the phone from Upsalla, I hadn't the foggiest idea about Tom's possible relationship with Martin Wickman. My informant confided these things to me much later. So for the time being we must leave him as an anonymous entity.

According to Tom's narrative after he got back to Stockholm, for he did get back to Stockholm after all, as the story will unfold, the vehicle used by the gangsters was one of these windowless vans which make it virtually impossible for passengers sitting in them to see one another. Even the windscreen and tiny side openings on either side of the front seat were made of thick coloured glass which, though allowing the driver to see objects outside the van, made it impossible for objects inside the van to be seen from outside. Apart from the door near the driver's seat there was only one other door at the back which could be opened by sliding part of the van's body upwards.

After Linda and Tom had been ordered into the van at gun point, they were pushed to the back seat which was in fact, no more than a bench of hard wood fixed on the floor of the van. Two thugs sat on the back seat; one on either side of the two captives, while the driver who appeared to be the youngest of the group, did the driving.

They had driven for about twenty minutes when the van slowed down and one of the thugs sitting close to Tom opened the back door and ordered Tom to get out. He himself also went outside the van carrying his gun. He closed the door of the van thus precluding the possibility of those in the van seeing what was happening outside.

It was a lonely wooded spot, and Tom thought his end had arrived, for this was as good a spot as anybody could have chosen to dispose of an unwanted individual. To Tom's great surprise, the man pushed a few Swedish crowns into Tom's hand and whispered, "Your fare to Stockholm." He then motioned to Tom to move and stand behind the van; and aiming his gun at a distant tree, he fired his gun once. Then he entered the van, and they drove off.

Tom stood by the roadside wondering what all that meant. He guessed that the firing of the gun must have meant to scare Linda into believing that he, Tom, had been shot dead.

Tom wasn't sure if going back to Stockholm as advised by the gangster was the best thing to do. He had come to Lulea at the invitation of Mr. Wickman. He had been warmly welcomed by the millionaire and his family, and no doubt, he had great expectations too! It would definitely be unbecoming for him to run away after this mishap without informing Mr. Wickman about it.

So, he made up his mind to return to Mr. Wickman. But how to get there! He wasn't sure of his directions. What with the tall trees on either side of the road, he couldn't make out in which direction Lulea was. It was now getting close to sun set and for a fraction of a second he was seized by fear. What would happen to him if he did not get help? Where would he spend the night?

While he was thus pondering his situation, he heard the sound of an oncoming motor vehicle. Presently a tractor loaded with hay appeared up the road, and Tom frantically motioned to the driver to stop. The old farmer unexpectedly seeing a black man standing by the roadside hesitated a bit and made as if he was proceeding without stopping. Tom's heart sank, as he shouted, "Please, please, stop and listen to me!"

The driver slowly brought the old tractor to a stop and Tom briefly poured out his predicament to the old farmer. Fortunately there was no language problem between them, as virtually all Swedes have at least a working knowledge of English, thanks to an enlightened education policy which requires every Swedish child to learn English at school. Tom briefly told the old farmer that he wished to go to Mr. Martin Wickman of Lulea, without going into the details of his story.

"Lulea?" asked the old farmer. "That's easy. It is only twenty kilometres away. Come, sit here beside me," he said showing Tom a nook on the tractor on which was fastened a dirty foam cushion. Tom clambered on to the tractor.

They drove in silence for two odd kilometres, and the farmer swerved on to a side dirt road. Within a few minutes they entered a neatly kept farm with several buildings dotting it. It appeared from the look of things, that this man was a dairy farmer; for the first building they came to was a large stable built of red brick. There was no doubt in Tom's mind that this farmer was a prosperous one; and indeed he was, for he himself told Tom after they had settled down over cheese and biscuits in his wooden house two hundred metres from the stable, that he had seventy five dairy cattle and that his monthly turn over from the sale of milk averaged about 1 million SEK.

Mr. Lunn the farmer had time to take a bath and have a change of clothes. He then joined Tom in the sitting room and introduced his wife Lisa to Tom. There seemed to be no young people in the house, and Tom assumed rightly, that the old couple's children must all be grown ups leading lives of their own elsewhere in Sweden or abroad.

It was while they were munching cheese and biscuits in the sitting room that Tom unfolded his full story to Mr. Lunn: how he had been invited by Mr. Wickman; how he and Linda had been abducted; and how he had subsequently been set free at the spot Mr. Lunn had picked him.

The kind Mr. Lunn understood the seriousness of Tom's story, and the name of Martin Wickman made it imperative that he should render immediate assistance to Tom. So, without wasting time, Mr. Lunn kissed his wife goodbye, went to the garage, and started the brand new Volvo. Tom bade farewell to Mrs. Lunn and clambered into the luxurious car. Within fifteen minutes they were in the streets of Lulea.

Mr. Wicknan's villa, or castle to be more exact, stood on a promontory jutting into the Gulf of Bothnia, which is the northern part of the Baltic Sea. It is said that this castle belonged to the Swedish kings in the distant past, but the Swedish royalty now having lost some of its former glory, some of its estates and castles had also got lost along the way. The story goes that this particular castle was auctioned off some years ago by the royal family, and now Mr. Wickman was its proud owner. He had, of course, carried out major repairs and modifications to make it look modern and attractive. The whole estate covering about ten acres, consisted of a golf course, a swimming pool, lovely lawns, flowers, shrubs, pine trees, stables, worker's quarters, and the main castle buildings. Indeed, Mr. Wickman's abode, according to Tom's description, was paradise on earth, if we can allow ourselves the license of using this blessed word.

Mr. Lunn stopped his Volvo on the drive way just in front of the main entrance to the castle.

"Here you are, sir," Mr. Lunn said turning to look at Tom, "Mr. Wickman's place."

"I don't know how to thank you, sir," Tom said, rummaging in his pocket to fish out the money he had been given by one of the kidnappers. But Mr. Lunn waved him off when he saw the money, saying, "T'was my pleasure to help you. Keep the money and use it for something else. After all, you Tanzanians are good people. See, my own son worked in Tanzania for four years, and he used to speak very highly of you. He's back in Sweden now working in the SIDA office in Stockholm."

While this conversation was going on, Gregesen, one of several valets administering to Mr. Wickman, approached the car, and Mr. Lunn spoke to him briefly. The valet opened the door of the car to let Tom out. Seeing Tom outside the car, Gregesen recognised him as the guest staying at the castle. So he was all smiles as he welcomed Tom. "Hey, sir, you've been gone a long time since lunch. Mr. Wickman was asking about you. How about Miss Wickman, where's she?"

Tom simply said, "Can you take me to Mr. Wickman right now? I must speak to him at once. Something's happened to Miss Wickman and I must report to him."

Gregesen asked Tom to follow him into Mr. Wickman's study, and Mr. Lunn decided to follow them in order, if necessary, to corroborate at least part of Tom's narrative to Mr. Wickman.

Mr. Wickman was found in his study poring over his books. He was fond of reading; especially reading about mineral prospecting. When Gregesen entered the study, Mr. Wickman's first impulse was to object to this uncalled for intrusion into his privacy in the strongest possible terms. But when he saw both Tom and Lunn following close behind Gregesen, common sense dictated that he should restrain his anger.

"Hey, Tom," Mr. Wickman said as soon as he saw him. "I was wondering what'd happened. We agreed you'd say goodbye to us at 17 hours before Linda drove you to the airport to catch the evening flight to Stockholm. Did you miss the flight? And where's Linda?" Mr. Wickman asked in one breath.

"I am afraid, sir, I have bad news to tell you," Tom answered. "Linda and I were abducted by three hooded thugs at gun point. I was set free after some time, but Linda was spirited away." Tom stopped for a while to let the message sink in the millionaire's mind.

Mr. Wickman adjusted his glasses, took a small packet from his trouser pocket and swallowed a tiny tablet he always carried with him. Mr. Wickman was a known case of hypertension, but due to strict adherence to his doctor's advice as to his diet, physical exercises, and the regular use of anti-hypertensive drugs, he had managed to live with this condition for many years. He knew now that this kind of information could easily trigger a rise of his B.P. That's why he fortified himself first thing on hearing the bad news.

"When did that happen?" He asked, not knowing exactly where to begin.

"Sir, soon after lunch I went to my room for a short rest. Linda had arranged to give me a conducted tour of the estate beginning at 2 p.m. So at about that time we started off exploring the grounds. We visited the swimming pool and the sauna; we crossed the golf course, and examined plants in the green house. From there we went to the flower garden near the pine forest. It must have been around 4 p.m. when we started off along the narrow road which leads to the horse shed intending to return to the castle, so I could bid you farewell as arranged, before Linda drove me to the airport.

"Suddenly two hooded men sprang from the shrubs, guns pointing at us, and bade us to walk silently to a van carefully parked behind a shrub. We entered the van and they drove us away. It was so dark inside that cursed van, we could hardly see a thing. They drove us for something like half an hour and then they stopped the van, ordered me out of the van at a lonely place I knew not which, and they drove off with Linda."

Mr. Lunn picked up the story from there and said, "It was at Lundberg they left him. You know I live on my farm at Lundberg. Lunn's my name".

"You, Lunn Gottberg?" asked Mr. Wickman.

"Yeah, Lunn Gottberg."

"I know your farm; been there as a matter of fact. Remember I took some American farmers to your farm two years ago? They wanted to see an example of a good Swedish dairy farm?"

"Of course, I remember," answered Mr. Lunn. "Well, I found him standing by the road side, only two kilometres from my farm, as I was returning from collecting hay. When I saw him frantically waving at me to stop, I had half a mind to proceed without stopping in order to avoid possible trouble. But something inside me told me to stop, and I decided to bring him over."

While listening to Tom's narrative and to Lunn Gottberg's corroborative details, Mr. Wickman was visibily moved. He perspired a little and kept mopping his forehead.

"What do these people want from me?" Mr. Wickman soliloquized. "I've done everything for this country. What else do they want me to do? Why pick on my daughter? Why pick on me? Are'nt there other millionaires is Sweden?" Then turning to Mr. Lunn he asked, "Well, Gottberg, what's your advice? What should I do? What can I do?"

"I think," Mr. Lunn answered, "the best thing is for you to keep cool for the moment. If it's money or anything else they're after, they will soon make their demand known. They cannot have simply wanted to draw blood. If that had been their intention they would have simply bumped your daughter off when they saw her. They would not have set him free, either," Mr. Lunn reasoned, pointing his finger at Tom. He continued, "If, as this gentleman says, one of the thugs, the one who fired a shot to scare Linda, gave him money for his fare to Stockholm, you may take it from me that these people have a soft spot somewhere in their collective conscience."

"Oh, he gave you money, did he?" asked Mr. Wickman directing his gaze to Tom.

"Yes, this is what he gave me," Tom answered, fishing the Swedish crowns from his pocket.

"It sounds like you're right, Gottberg. They could be the kind of people who might leave my daughter unharmed if I could meet their demands. But what *are* their demands?" Mr. Wickman asked rhetorically.

"As I was saying," said Mr. Lunn, "we must wait until the demands are known. It's getting on to 8 p.m. and I told Lisa I would be back soon. If you will excuse me I must push off. If I can be of any service, please let met know. Here's my telephone number." Mr. Lunn said while scribbling his telephone number on a piece of paper. He said goodbye to Mr. Wickman and Tom, and Gregesen escorted him to his car.

While this conversation had been going on in Mr. Wickman's study, Mrs Wickman had been elsewhere in the castle. Mr. Wickman then asked Tom to accompany him to one of the many sitting rooms in the castle where they found Mrs. Wickman watching her favourite television programme. It was a small, but very cosy sitting room which, Tom was told, was used exclusively by Mr. and Mrs. Wickman.

In a few emotional words, Mr. Wickman broke the bad news to his wife, and then asked Tom to describe the details. Tom obliged by going through the story again, while Linda's mother was sobbing quietly. She was a courageous woman; for, having heard the story she said, "I thank God that they spared you. I shudder to think what would have happened if they had taken you with Linda. Not only would it have strained Sweden's relationship with Tanzania, but the endowment we agreed to leave you, would have come to nothing. As for my daughter, I pray that they let us know their demands." Turning to her husband she said, "Martin, we must do anything to save Linda."

Having said that, she stood up and slowly walked to her bedroom while Mr. Wickman and Tom returned to the study where Mr. Wickman made a number of telephone calls. As the conversation was in Swedish Tom could not follow what was being said, but he guessed Mr. Wickman was informing all the important people he thought could play a part in saving Linda's life.

From the study they both went to the dining room where Gregesen was waiting to serve them dinner. But both Mr. Wickman and Tom ate very little. Mrs Wickman did not even appear in the dining room.

6

By 9 am on Monday, no word had been received from the kidnappers. Mr. and Mrs. Wickman were glued to their Xerox Fax machine. The strain was almost palpable. At 10.30 am the long awaited communication from the kidnappers came through in the form of a faxed message signed by Linda Wickman. It read:-

"Dear Father,

Tom and I were abducted by three hooded men yesterday afternoon while I was showing Tom round the estate. They later ordered Tom out of the van, but I fear they may have shot him, for, I heard a single shot before the man who had gone out with Tom re-entered the van.

"They are holding me in a small log cabin in Abisko National park in the county of Kiruna, not very far from the Norwegian border.

"I have not been able to see the face of any of these people, as they wear nylon masks or hoods all the time. It appears they live in another cabin nearby, for I am all alone in my cabin where they have tied me to a pole. There is in my cabin a supply of dry bread and water enough to last me a few days. There is also somebody guarding my cabin outside; for I can hear him walking round the cabin, all the time.

"Important: these people demand 10 kilogrammes of solid gold, and 10 kilogrammes of rubies. They must get the treasure on Thursday this week. Only one vehicle carrying the ransom treasure should enter the gate leading into the park at 2 p.m. this Thursday. The vehicle shall be driven half a kilometer into the park, to the point where the road ends. The person carrying the treasure shall strip himself naked, except for tight pants, and leave his clothes in the vehicle. He will carry the treasure and walk about 100 metres down hill to the first igloo shaped cabin on the right hand side of the footpath. He should leave the treasure in that cabin.

"He should then continue another 100 metres down the slope to yet another lonely cabin where he will find me. Both of us will then leave, taking a different footpath to the vehicle, and drive off.

"They have told me to emphasize the following: as soon as the treasure is left in the first cabin, one of them will enter the cabin to verify the authenticity of the gold and rubies, and weigh them using a weighing machine hidden in the cabin. This man will be in communication with the other gangsters by means of a walkie talkie. The discovery of any fake minerals or of a missing ounce of each of the minerals will mean the immediate death of both the courier and myself.

"They have further stressed that the courier should try no tricks, for, from the moment he will leave the vehicle after entering the national park, he will be covered by two powerful telescopic rifles which hardly ever miss their targets. Also, if they detect any sign of police surveillance, as in the form of a helicopter flying overhead near this area; or in the form of an unknown person being spotted in this area, they will destroy me. Mind you, these people are scanning the area using very powerful binoculars.

"Father, do what you can to save me. Do as they say, and I'll be safe. Kisses to mummy.

Love,
Linda."

Mr. and Mrs. Wickman read and re-read the faxed message until they could almost recite it by heart. This was mid Monday morning. The deadline was only seventy hours away. Speed was therefore of essential importance. Damn these thugs! If only they had demanded money, two million SEK, for instance, the Swedish millionaire would have found the money without the slightest difficulty. But solid gold and rubies!

True, Mr. Wickman did own gold mines at Mpepo and Lukalasi in Mbinga district, and ruby mines at Matombo and Mahenge in Morogoro region, but that did not mean he had hoarded gold and rubies in his castle in Lulea. According to Swedish law, all valuable minerals like gold, and gemstones like rubies had to be deposited in the vaults of the Central Bank. Of course, the owner of any such valuables could, at any time, get money from the Central Bank up to the total worth of the gold or gemstones deposited with the Bank. But on no account should citizens hoard these things in their homes. Goldsmiths and jewellers holding valid licenses could buy their raw materials from the Central Bank, but the amounts sold were carefully rationed.

But the Wickmans were neither goldsmiths nor jewellers, and the thought that one day they might have to pay the ransom of their daughter in terms of solid gold and rubies never crossed their minds. So how does Mr. Wickman get these treasures within seventy hours? This was no matter to be settled over the phone. So ringing the President of the Central Bank was out of the question. Mr. Wickman had to see the Bank President in person.

Now, in his great hurry to get things organized so that he could fly to Stockholm in his three seater Cessna to confer with the President of the Central Bank, Mr. Wickman inadvertently forgot the faxed message from Linda on a table in the study, while he busied himself sorting out other papers in his bedroom.

Gregesen who had seen the message on the table nodded maliciously, and with the speed of lightning he got hold of the piece of paper and had the message photocopied using the Xerox photocopier on another table nearby. He quickly replaced the original exactly where he had picked it from. He pocketed the copy and walked out of the study. He was sure if he played his cards right he would make some money by selling that sensational news item to one of the local papers.

Gregesen who was a Dane by nationality, had dropped out of school at the age of fifteen. Since then he had spent ten years doing odd jobs in Copenhagen, sometimes working as a porter at the International Airport, and sometimes cleaning plates in restaurants, until he was able to save enough money to enable him pay his boat fare to Gotteborg, Sweden, where again he managed to get menial, but better paid jobs in hotels.

He lived in Gotterborg for five years before moving on to Stockholm, and later to Lulea where he secured his present job as Mr. Wickman's valet. By the time the events chronicled here took place, Gregesen had been with the Wickmans for ten years. He was now over forty years old, but still unmarried.

It's one of those common human fallacies to assume that unmarried valets who spend a whole decade serving a millionaire, cannot conceive the idea of breaking away to lead independent lives of their own. So it was with the Wickmans. They took it for granted that Gregesen was so dependent on them that he would never dream of deserting them. Little did they know that Gregesen had, in fact, made up his mind to return to Denmark to marry his childhood friend with whom he had kept lively, if not amorous, correspondence through the years.

It is, again, one of those paradoxes of life that very often, rich people of the multi-millionaire category treat their personal attendants like objects who do not need advancement in their social status. Such was the case with Mr. Wickman. Although Gregesen had worked for him faithfully for ten years, Mr. Wickman had never raised his salary beyond the minimum permissible for valets in Sweden. In his estimation Mr. Wickman thought that the free meals Gregesen was getting at the castle and the other social amenities he was enjoying, more than compensated for any rise in salary. But human nature, especially male human nature, does no behave that way. A man wants to feel independent and responsible for his own life. A man would rather live independently in his own cottage, providing the necessities of life to his family, than be condemned to a life of serfdom in a king's palace! Had Mr. Wickman known this basic fact about male human nature he might not have taken Gregesen for granted as his eternal servant!

At 1.30 p.m. the Wickmans and Tom took off for Stockholm in the three seater Cessna. On arrival at the airport outside Stockholm, one of Mr. Wickman's assistants living in Stockholm drove them to a high class suburban area where they spent the night in a beautiful villa. The fully furnished three bedroom villa with a spacious living room, dining room, garage and other physical amenities stood on half an acre of prime land which was enclosed by a fence of reinforced concrete and steel bars.

At 9 a.m. on Tuesday soon after breakfast, the Wickmans called Tom into the sitting room, and there in the presence of Mr. Olaf Olsen, assistant to Mr. Wickman, and Mr. John Johanson a city solicitor whom Mr. Wickman had invited specifically for this occasion, Tom was given a number of papers to sign. Copies of the papers were given to the city solicitor and Mr. Olsen, while the originals were given to Tom. These were official documents transferring the ownership of the villa and everything in it, and the piece of land on which the villa stood, from Mr. Wickman to Tom Nyirenda. This was part of the endowment that Mrs. Wickman had referred to the other day when she said that if Tom had disappeared with Linda the endowment would have come to nothing. So when Tom had hinted in his office in Dar that there was more to the visit to Sweden than the signing of an agreement which would lead to the launching of the NCSSD, this is what he had meant: he would, while in Sweden, be handed a fully furnished luxury villa as a present for services rendered to Mr. Wickman!

Tom was ceremoniously handed all the keys of the house and the gate, as a formal symbol of ownership of the property. He held them for a few minutes while Mr. Olsen took some photographs, and then handed them to Mr. Johanson. It had been pre-arranged that with effect from the moment Mr. Johanson, the solicitor received the keys, the house would be leased to a certain law firm which Mr. Johanson represented. From then on the president of the law firm would occupy the house. The rent had all been worked out in advance, and it had been agreed that an advance down payment covering the first six month's rent payable in USD be paid into Tom's Foreign Account which the Solicitor would help Tom in opening. As a matter of fact, some of the papers Tom had signed had to do with this question of leasing the house to the law firm.

This was indeed a windfall for Tom. His great expectations had come true. For a while Tom forgot the problem the Wickmans were in. Indeed, he momentarily forgot Linda. He shuddered to think what would have happened if the thugs had bumped him off. All these developments would have come to nothing as Mrs. Wickman had put it. He thanked his stars.

* * * * *

As soon as the Wickmans and Tom left the castle for Lulea airport that Monday afternoon, Gregesen went to the garage and started the old van which he often used to buy provisions in town. He drove straight to the offices of the *Lulea Herald,* one of the top ten papers in Sweden. He walked into the news room and asked to see the news editor, Mr. Paul Betelsen. Having been ushered in Mr. Betelsen's office, Gregesen began his bargain without wasting time.

"Sir," he said, "I have an important news item to sell."

"What's it?" asked the editor.

"It's about a kidnap which happened yesterday."

"A kidnap, did you say?"

"Yes."

"Who's the victim?"

"I can't begin telling you things before we strike a bargain."

"What bargain?"

"You agree to buy my story. I can assure you it's going to be the most sensational story in all Sweden, if you publish it."

"Look here, old chap, you either tell me who's been kidnapped, or you leave my office. I have no time to waste. As you can see, we are very busy here. Every minute we get either telephone calls, or fax messages, telexes, reports, or we get visitors who come in person to report news to us."

Gregesen produced his identity card and showed it to the editor. The card had his passport size photograph affixed on it, and below the photograph was his name and the caption, 'Wickman's valet'. Below the caption was Mr. Wickman's signature superimposed over the stamp of the castle.

Now everybody in Lulea knew the castle. It was the only one in Lulea, and all the important citizens of Lulea, especially the bankers and newspaper editors knew Mr. Wickman's signature. So when Mr. Betelsen examined Gregesen's identity card, he was sure it had been signed by the Lulea millionaire.

"Sir, I'm Mr. Wickman's valet. Been with him for ten years," Gregesen said.

"Yes, I can see Mr. Wickman's signature. So what's the news? Who's been kidnapped?"

"His daughter, Linda. Here's the fax message Linda sent to Mr.Wickman. It lays down the kidnapper's demands before they can release her," Gregesen said, waving the fax message before the curious newspaper editor.

Gregesen knew that the message said Tom had probably been shot, but he also knew that Tom hadn't been shot. To allow this information to be published as it was, meant purposely giving untrue information to the press, which was unethical. So what should Gregesen do? Should he tell Betelsen that although the message was genuine, in that it had originated from the kidnappers, that part of it which said that Linda's companion may have been shot, should be omitted since Tom was still alive after all? But surely if he said this, Mr. Betelsen was sure to throw him out of his office, and to throw the piece of paper into the waste paper basket because he would regard it as a hoax. In any case, to reveal this truth about Tom would be to dampen the sensationality of the story.

Mr. Betelsen now looked at Gregesen with the interest of a cat looking at a fat mouse. He said, "Well now, Mr. Gregesen, how much do you want for your story?"

"Two thousand SEK."

"Oh, no, we never pay that much for any story."

"OK. Then I will try another newspaper. But I'm sure you'll regret having missed this hot cake. Mind you, Mr. Wickman himself doesn't know I've brought the message here. He didn't want the news leaked to the press here in Lulea, but I'm sure he is going to have it published by one of the Stockholm papers where he flew a short while ago. The news will probably appear in the Stockholm papers the day after tomorrow. If you buy this thing from me now, your paper will be the only one to carry the story tomorrow."

While Gregesen was thus persuading the editor, Mr. Betelsen was thinking what a sensational story it would make to describe the kidnapping of the millionaire's daughter. He already imagined people jostling at news stands to get copies of the *Lulea Herald.* He made up his mind.

"Alright, Mr. Gregesen," he said, "we'll give you two thousand SEK." So saying he fished from his table drawer crisp notes worth two thousand SEK and bought Gregesen's fax message after studying it in detail.

* * * * *

In Stockholm that Tuesday morning, Tom and Mr. Johnson, the solicitor, drove to a nearby bank to open a bank account for Tom while Mr. Olsen drove Mr. and Mrs. Wickman to the president of the Central Bank of Sweden. The Central Bank building was a huge twelve storey structure built of the most modern and most expensive building materials.

For a lesser mortal it would have been next to impossible to see the Bank president at a moment's notice, but when the name of Wickman was mentioned by the president's assistant, it took only five minutes for the Lulea millionaire and his wife to be ushered into the president's office on the eighth floor.

Mr. Kenth Larson, the Bank president, welcomed the Wickmans cordially but with expressions of sympathy. He said, "I'm sorry, Martin, for what has happened to your daughter."

Both Mr. Wickman and his wife were confused.

"So you know the story already?" Mr. Wickman asked.

"Of course. It's all in the *Lulea Herald*. Haven't you read it?" So saying, Kenth Larson fished a copy of the *Lulea Herald* from a pile of different newspapers on his desk and handed it to Mr. Wickman. Yes, there it was on the front page of the Herald in exceptionally big letters, "MILLIONAIRE'S DAUGHTER ABDUCTED". The article quoted verbatim the letter sent by Linda to her father. It went on to make an impassioned plea to the Central Bank to issue Mr. Wickman with the required ransom treasure in order to save Linda's life. It pointed out the many philanthropic services that the Lulea millionaire had rendered to Sweden generally, and to Lulea in particular.

There was only one flaw in the article. It was reported that Linda's African companion had probably been shot dead, when, in fact, Tom was at that very moment probably getting his new cheque book from some Scandinavian bank!

Apart from this flaw, Mr. Wickman felt the publication of the story could be a blessing in disguise. It might help whip up public opinion in his favour, and one could not rule out the extraordinary influence of public opinion in such cases. Even so, Mr. Wickman was at a loss to know how the story could have leaked to the press. He wondered aloud, "How the hell did the *Lulea Herald* get this story?"

"You mean you didn't give the information to the press?" asked Mr. Larson.

"Not at all."

"Well, someone must have talked to the press," said Mr. Larson.

"Could it be Lunn Gottberg?" Martin Wickman asked his wife.

"It can't be him," Mrs. Wickman answered. "Lunn could not have said that Linda's companion had probably been shot when he is the one who brought Tom to the castle. Besides, don't you see that this is a verbatim reproduction of the message from Linda?"

"Then who could have sent the message to the press? Could it be the kidnappers themselves? See, I have here the fax message sent to me by Linda," Mr. Wickman said, giving the fax message to the Bank president.

While Mr. Larson was studying the message, Mrs. Wickman said, "I've a strong suspicion it could have been Gregesen."

"But how could it have been him when I had the message with me all the time?"

"Are you sure you had it with you all the time?" Mrs. Wickman asked. "I didn't see you pick it from the desk in the study after you'd sorted the other papers in the bedroom. Martin, you must have left it on the desk for sometime."

"Even so, when did Gregesen send it to the press?"

"You're getting old, Martin. Can't you see that Gregesen could easily have photocopied it? The photocopier is on the other table nearby. If you carelessly left the message on the desk, what could have prevented him from photocopying it?" Insisted Mrs. Wickman.

"But what would he have done that for?" Mr. Wickman asked.

"To sell it to the press, as he most probably did."

"Oh, I see. You may be right, darling."

"Mr. Larson had finished reading the fax message. He looked up at Wickman and asked, "Is this what brings you here, Martin?"

"This is what brings me here, Kenth. As you can see, you are the only person in the whole wide world who can help me out of this jam."

"I certainly feel we must help you out. But I have to speak to the Prime Minister first. You know that's what the law says. I'll try to convince him, alright."

"Mr. Kenth Larson left the office and went into an inner chamber where there was a special hot line used for special purposes only. After a while he returned smiling. "The Prime Minister," he said, "has read the article in today's *Lulea Herald*, and he sends you his warmest sympathies for the misfortune. He says he has been waiting to hear from you since morning, but you didn't ring him. He says he is prepared to use all the State power at his disposal to bring the terrorists to book if you so wish. But when he heard what I had to say, he understood that you prefer treating the matter quietly as a family affair. He has approved your request that we issue you with the ransom treasure. You've deposited enough gold and gemstones to meet the demands of the kidnappers; still the Bank will have to charge you commission on the service to be rendered."

"We are extremely grateful for your consideration, and please convey our heart felt gratitude to the Prime Minister," Mr. Wickiman said.

"Now, Martin," the Bank President said, "we have to agree on the timing for carrying out the operation. I mean the time for removing the treasure from the vaults and handing it over to you, and so on. This will enable me to line up the people required to carry out the operation. You see, even a Bank President like myself, cannot take anything from the vaults all by himself. To open the various locks to the vaults you require at least four people, including myself, of course. But you require the chief of the metropolitan police, the paymaster general and others. It's not easy to line up such people, you know."

"Well," said Mr. Wickman, "this is Tuesday. We've only tomorrow and part of Thursday at our disposal. I was thinking of using my light three seater Cessna to fly the treasure to Kiruna on Thursday. It would take three hours to fly to Kiruna. Olsen would start off to Kiruna tomorrow, driving one of my bullet proof cars, and be at Kiruna airport ready to receive the treasure on our arrival. It takes approximately two hours to drive form Kiruna to Abisko National park. All this means that we require a minimum of five hours between getting the treasure from the Bank and depositing it at 2 p.m. in that cursed cabin of theirs. So the latest time I should get the treasure is 9 a.m. Thursday."

"Let's make it 8 a.m. to be on the safe side," said Mrs. Wickman.

"I agree with you," said Mr. Larson. Eight o'clock is a more convenient time than nine o'clock. I'll arrange for one of our special bullet proof vans to be used for the movement of the treasure to the airport."

Mr. Larson then went on to describe in detail how the operation would be carried out: where the entrance to the vaults was; where Mr. Wickman's car would wait; how Mr. Wickman would identify the bullet proof van as it would emerge from the underground vaults, and so on.

Then Mr. Larson asked a number of pertinent questions. "Who's going to pilot the plane?" He asked.

"I mean to do it myself."

"That sounds reasonable; and who's going to drive you to the airport?"

"My wife will drive me and the courier to the airport. After the courier and myself have taken off, she will return to the city."

"Good; and who's leaving for Kiruna tomorrow?"

"My assistant Olsen."

"I see, and who's actually going to carry the treasure to the cabin? I mean who is the courier who is accompanying you on the plane?"

"Mr. Wickman hesitated. He hadn't seriously thought about that. "I must confess," he said, "I haven't given it serious thought yet."

"What?" Mr. Larson asked in astonishment. "You haven't thought of the person who will be the target of powerful telescopic rifles? My dear Martin, this is the person you should have thought about more than anybody else. As a matter of fact, this is not the person you should choose, but one who should offer to carry out the mission. You need a courageous person, and you must be ready to reward him handsomely. You see, the slightest mistake by this person could bring the whole thing to a sad end. In such situations the actors on both sides become edgy. For instance, your man carrying the treasure could slip accidentally and fall down while walking to the first cabin. The thugs covering him with rifles might mistake that for a trick the courier was trying to play, and one or both of them might pull the trigger. Excuse my inquisitiveness, Martin, but I thought I should get you to think about these things carefully. Please do think about your courier carefully, today."

The Wickmans thanked Mr. Larson and he escorted them to his private lift. Mr. Olsen who had been waiting for them all along, drove them first to Tom's villa, which had now been leased to Mr. Johanson's law firm. There they met both the solicitor Johanson and Tom Nyirenda who had returned earlier from opening a bank account. The Wickmans collected Tom, and Olsen drove them to Diplomat Hotel.

7

The Wickmans and Tom had lunch at Diplomat Hotel. After lunch they sat together in the hotel lobby and Mr. Wickman apprised Tom of the developments reached with the President of the Central Bank. But when he came to the crucial problem of having to find a person who would volunteer to carry out the mission of delivering the treasure to the gangsters, he was visibly disturbed.

"To tell you the truth, Tom, I don't know anybody I can approach to do this difficult assignment. I could, of course, have it advertised in the papers. "Wanted a courier to deliver ransom treasure to terrorists hiding in Abisko National Park", or something like that, or I could arrange to appear on television and make an impassioned plea for assistance, but to do any of these things would be to court more trouble. Who knows if I wouldn't end up losing both the treasure and my daughter? No, I don't want to do that. I prefer going about it quietly as a family affair. I would, of course, be prepared to pay the volunteer handsomely once the mission had been accomplished successfully."

"Let's give ourselves some time to think about it," Tom suggested. He went on, "I would like to go to our Embassy to assure my people that I'm still alive. Having read this story they must be worrying to death about finding my dead body; and who knows if they haven't already spoken to Dar es Salaam and probably broken the news to my wife? While I'm there I will discuss with someone I trust about this problem of finding a willing and reliable courier."

"Good luck, Tom," Mr. Wickman said. "Try what you can, and contact me later this afternoon. We will drop you at the Tanzanian Embassy and proceed to Hilton Hotel where we'll spend the night. You can ring Hilton Hotel and ask for me."

* * * * *

David Chambakare and myself said goodbye to Professor Samwelson and entered the car to start the two hour drive to Stockholm. The man from SIDA headquarters who was driving us knew that we were in no mood for conversation, so he was not as talkative as he had been the day we came to Upsalla when he drew our attention to every interesting feature we passed: small longitudinal lakes scooped by glaciers during the great ice age; end moraines left behind by the retreating ice; beautiful forests, wheat farms, industrial complexes, and so on. This time he simply concentrated on the wheel.

Our friend, Tom, had probably been shot dead. His body hadn't been found yet. Minister Msokonde was waiting for us at Ambassador Mhina's residence. What were we going to discuss there? Was our visit to Sweden going to be cut short because of these events? I looked at David while the driver was pressing the accelerator pedal rather hard, but David was in no mood to chatter. He had told me back home in Dar that he had been to Sweden before. I was sure, although he hadn't told me so, that he had his own private plans to visit his former friends as soon as our official engagements came to an end Friday evening, when the Swedish Minister for Lands and

Environment would host a party in honour of our delegation. Our departure for Dar was scheduled for the following Monday morning. So we were to have two clear days when we would be left to our own devices. I was sure David intended to put those two days to maximum use. But now these developments! Curse these terrorists, and curse Tom, even though he was now probably rotting in some forest somewhere!

We drove in silence most of the time except for the occasional remark made by one of us when he spotted a wild animal or a strange looking bird. After two hours we were in the outskirts of Stockholm, and I asked the driver to leave us at the Tanzanian embassy from where we would be taken to the Ambassador's residence by the Embassy staff.

* * * * *

We were sitting round a table in the sitting room of Ambassor Mhina's residence: Minister Msokonde, Ambassador Mhina, Mr. Chuma the counsellor, Mrs. Mbapila, the first Secretary, David Chambakare and myself. We were discussing Tom's death in earnest. Proposals and counter proposals were being made: should we break the news to Dar? Should we demand an official explanation from the Swedish Government? Should we persuade the Swedish government to assist in looking for the body? How about compensation, should we demand some kind of compensation from the Swedish Government? If by chance the body was found, who should be responsible for transporting it home?

At one point Mr. Msokonde who was chairing the meeting lost his temper and started shouting at us, "You people should feel ashamed of yourselves. You come to a foreign country and begin getting mixed up with women. When you get killed, we all have to bear the consequences; and not only us, but our country is put to shame!"

Ambassador Mhina who was far wiser and more intelligent than the Minister calmed him down and said, "What you say is true and reasonable. But at the moment this moralizing will not help us. What we need is to concentrate on what line of action to take right now."

David said, "Certainly breaking the news to Dar es Salaam at this point in time is not advisable. If the body were found, yes; then we would have no alternative."

While David was thus speaking, there was a knock on the door, and in walked Tom Nyirenda, wearing an immaculately white *kanzu*. Everybody, except myself, stood from their chairs intending to run away, for they all believed they were seeing a ghost. I did not stir from my seat, knowing that this was Tom Nyirenda, alright. I knew that Tom had several of these *kanzus* which he occasionally used to wear in the evenings at private family gatherings at home. But I guess none of those present in the room had ever seen Tom in this garb. Even I did not know that he had brought a *kanzu* with him on this trip. I knew Tom to be fond of playing jokes at times, and when I saw him enter, I knew he had donned this *kanzu* precisely to scare us into believing that we were seeing his ghost, or that he had risen from the dead.

"Peace, ho!" he said, extending his arms. "It's I, fear not," he continued, imitating biblical language. He looked for a chair and sat down while I burst out laughing. Everybody else returned to his seat and joined in the laughing, except Peter Msokinde, the Minister. He was furious. He said, "Mr. Nyirenda, you may be older than myself, but your behaviour leaves much to be desired. I can tell you right away that the President will have to decide whether to leave you in the Ministry and remove me, or vice versa. I will certainly not feel comfortable working with you any more."

"As you please," answered Tom, lighting his Rothmans cigarette. "But why don't you allow me sometime to tell you what actually happened to me?"

"Yes, I think we're all interested to hear that," said Ambassador Mhina. Tom began, "I'm extremely sorry for the great anxiety and worry I must have caused you. You see, I left here Friday evening and flew to Lulea to visit a young nephew of mine who works in a computer firm there. I had arranged to visit him before I left Dar. In fact, his mother, who is my sister, had asked me to take a present for him. I was pretty sure I'd be back here Sunday evening, ready for our official engagements on Monday. But on Sunday morning my nephew took me to the home of his fellow worker, the daughter of a wealthy gentleman who is, in fact, the main share holder of the firm Frank works for. My nephew's name is Frank Chirwa.

"While Frank's friend was showing us round her father's estate, these terrorists appeared and ordered the two of us into their van at gun point for reasons unknown to me. They didn't bother about young Frank. They left him alone but picked on me. I imagine they mistook me for Frank. When they later discovered the mistake they had made, they let me out of the van. I heard one of them saying, 'It's not him we were after; it's the chap we left behind'. So I was left at a place I knew not which, without a penny. I had to rely on good samaritans to give me lifts from place to place until I got to Stockhom this afternoon."

I knew all this to be a pack of lies, of course, but since Tom had said it, and it sounded plausible, we all tried to swallow it except Minister Msokonde.

He retorted, "But I hear that the woman actually came to Stockholm to collect you?"

"Oh, no," Tom answered. "If anybody saw me in the company of a lady on Friday evening, that lady was Babro Peterson. She works right here in Stockholm. She's the one who came to greet me at the airport on our day of arrival, you may still remember her. Well, Babro is the daughter of Mr. and Mrs. Peterson. They worked in Dar es Salaam for a number of years, and Mrs. Peterson used to teach at Jangwani Girls Secondary School. Babro was in the same class as my daughter Grace, and they were great friends. Last year Babro spent part of her leave with us in Dar. Last Friday, I had asked her to come to the hotel and take me to the airport."

Another pack of lies, but one which sounded convincing and probable to my colleagues. Even so, Msokonde stuck to his guns. He said he was cutting short his visit to Sweden and was returning to Dar es Salaam earlier than planned. He asked Mr. Mhina if the Embassy staff could arrange to change his booking so he could return to Dar by any available flight before Monday.

The meeting broke up in disarray. While Mr. Msokonde remained behind to sort out his travel arrangements, Tom, David and I returned to our rooms in Diplomat Hotel.

As soon as we had reached our rooms, Tom rang me, and I joined him in his room almost immediately. I knew he was now going to tell me the truth about his adventures of the past few days.

He poured me a small glass of sherry after making sure the door was securely locked.

"Did you believe that stuff I pumped into your ears at Mhina's place?" Tom asked me as he was sitting down facing me.

"Not a word of it," I answered.

Tom inserted a Rothmans cigarette into an expensive gilded cigarette holder, took an equally expensive cigarette lighter from his pocket, and lit up.

"Tom," I said pointing at the cigarette holder and lighter, "those are not the kind of things you buy while thumbing lifts from place to place as a penniless fugitive."

"Chris, how did Msokonde know that Linda came to take me from Stockholm? Did you tell him? You are the only one who saw me with Linda that Friday evening!"

"Certainly not me, Tom. I couldn't have told him that. When I spoke with Msokonde over the phone from Upsalla he did ask me if I knew the woman referred to in the newspaper article, and I flatly said I didn't."

"It could've been the girl at the reception counter. She saw me leave the hotel accompanied by Linda."

"Yeah, that's possible."

"Chris, I've come into some dough," Tom said, pulling out a stack of crisp dollar bills from the pocket of his *kanzu*, and throwing it into my laps. "Use that for your shopping," he said.

I counted the money and found I had enough to buy nice things for myself and my family.

"Thanks a lot, Tom," I said. "I can now return home and say I was in Sweden. Really, the so called travel allowance they give us back home when we go overseas is a big joke."

Then Tom began telling me the full story of the last few days since the time I left him with Linda in this very room. The story became particularly interesting when he came to the transfer of the Stockholm villa to him, and of course, the opening of the bank account.

I said I envied him for all that, but being his boyhood friend and his marriage godfather, I hoped that somehow I would also benefit from his windfall.

"What did you think about Msokonde's threats?" Tom asked me.

"Well, I wasn't sure if he meant what he was saying," I answered.

"Oh, yes, he was quite serious. I know him. That's how he behaves. I'm pretty sure that as soon as he gets home he will seek the earliest opportunity of seeing the President and pouring venom in his ears. But I can assure you, Chris, that I don't mind. In fact, if the worst comes to the worst, I will start the private business I've always been dreaming about - hotel business. You know my young brother Amos runs a small restaurant at Mikocheni. But if you've looked at that plot carefully you will have noticed there is ample space behind the restaurant. I acquired that huge plot for a purpose. I could decide to sell my property here in Stockholm; and I am sure the proceeds would be enough to enable me start a modest hotel business."

“You could employ me as hotel manager after I retire from ILD,” I joked. Tom laughed as he eased the cigarette stump from the holder and stubbed it out in an ashtray.

“But I tell you, Chris, if he really sees the President about this, it ‘ll be the end of him; for I’ll retaliate by revealing to the Chief Secretary all the goings on in that Ministry. He won’t stand a chance. I shudder to think what would become of him if he were dropped from the Cabinet. He would become a vagabond almost overnight. You see, that man doesn’t even own a house, and he has a large family. You know what government does when they remove you from office? They send a squad from Ujenzi to remove your belongings, within a week!”

“It’s a shame, isn’t it? Why do they do that?”

“Well, government regulations! But now, Chris, I’ve something more important to talk to you; this question of getting Linda from the claws of the terrorists. Mr. Wickman is desperately looking for somebody who will volunteer to be the courier to take the treasure to the terrorists. He is prepared to pay the courier handsomely if Linda can be delivered to him safely. I promised him I’d think about it, and contact him later today. My first impulse was to ask you to do it, but on second thoughts, I’m not sure if I should expose you to such peril. How do you feel about it? Mind you, the operation is fraught with danger. In such situations the actors on both sides become nervous. The slightest mistake you make could result in death. That’s why I do not want to encourage you too much.”

I looked at Tom, and with the wave of my hand I signaled to him to keep quiet while a prayer arose from my breast. I remembered my favorite Saint Michael the Archangel, but in particular, I found myself silently reciting Psalm 121. This is a Psalm I have recited countless times in my life, “*I will lift up mine eyes unto the hills….*” Yes, these terrorists would be aiming their guns at me from the hills of Abisko National Park, and I would lift up my eyes unto those hills. “*From whence comes my help?*” Where would my help come from in that remote unfamiliar place? “*My help cometh from the Lord who made heaven and earth.*” Yes, even in Abisko, my help would come from the self-same Lord.

I went on reciting the Psalm silently until I came to the crucial words, “*The Lord shall preserve thee from all evil; he shall preserve thy soul. The Lord shall preserve thy going out and thy coming in from this time forth, and even for evermore.*”

Tears welled up from my breast as I reflected on this last sentence of the Psalm. Tom was surprised to see me shedding silent tears. He said, "I'm sorry for having disturbed your peace of mind."

"No, you haven't disturbed my peace of mind. You have given me peace of mind, and I'm telling you, Tom, that I've made up my mind to carry out this assignment. I have an inner certitude that he who made heaven and earth will preserve me."

"In that case," Tom said, "let's go to Hilton Hotel right away."

I finished my sherry and we both left Tom's room. Outside Diplomat Hotel, we hailed a taxi which took us to Hilton Hotel, the most prestigious in Stockholm.

At the reception desk Tom asked to be put in touch with Mr. Wickman, and in a minute he was connected to him. He spoke with Mr. Wickman briefly on the phone, and we were directed to take the lift to the fifth floor where we found Mr. Wickman in room 515. Room 515 was really one of the several suites reserved only for the financial heavy weights. Within a minute we ensconced ourselves in a comfortable sitting room of the suite, and in subdued voices began to discuss details of the operation to come.

Tom first convinced Mr. Wickman that I was the right choice for the job, since I had whole heartedly volunteered to do it. Mr. Wickman readily agreed to accept me, not so much because he particularly liked my face, but I guess because he was so desperate, and there was really not much time left for him to find an alternative volunteer, short of appealing to the general public through television, a line of action he did not like to take.

So we went through the details of the operation. We started by going through the message faxed to Mr. Wickman to ensure that I knew the scenario by heart: stripping naked… carrying the treasure… entering first cabin… proceeding to second cabin… freeing Linda…. returning to car by different foot-path.

I was briefed on when I would be picked up from Diplomat Hotel to the airport on Thursday morning; where I would board the light aircraft to be piloted by Mr. Wickman himself; how at Kiruna airport Mr. Olsen and myself would carry the twenty kilograms of treasure to the bullet proof car which would be driven to Abisko National Park by Mr. Olsen. It was arranged that Mr. Wickman would be at Kiruna airport ready to fly Linda and myself to Lulea if all went well. It was also arranged that Mrs. Wickman would return to Lulea later on Thursday morning by a scheduled domestic flight.

8

The bullet proof van from the central bank carrying the ransom treasure and two armed police escorts, came to a stop barely a foot from the wing of Mr. Wickman's three seater Cessna. The Wickmans and myself had arrived five minutes earlier, at 8.30 to be exact. In a matter of minutes the two ten kilogram packages had been off loaded from the van, and locked in a compartment close to the pilot's seat. I clambered onto the aircraft and sat beside Mr. Wickman. We taxied for a few minutes and took off.

As soon as we reached cruising height, Mr. Wickman started talking about this and that, especially encouraging me to have steel nerves from the time I would enter the national park to the time I would re-enter the bullet proof car after freeing Linda. At times he reminisced on how he came to acquire the gold mines in Mbinga district, and asked me exactly what part of Mbinga district I came from, since he knew virtually every village in the district. I answered these innocent questions without hesitation; but when he resumed talking about the operation I was going to carry out, I pleaded with him to stop; for that kind of talk only helped to heighten my nervousness. He saw the point and changed to some other topics.

But what I really meant was to ask him to leave me alone to fortify myself with prayer. From the time of take off at Stockholm airport, I was mumbling silent prayers. I said all the prayers I knew, until finally I remembered what Father George A. Maloney says about prayer - contemplative prayer. Contemplative prayer, he says, should not mean making small speeches to God, rather it should simply be loving surrender to him. After all, we really do not know how to pray unless God's spirit teaches us how, or in fact, prays in us. When I came to this point I stopped saying this or that prayer, but simply surrendered myself into God's loving care.

Kiruma airport is an unassuming place with small looking airport buildings, but with excellent run ways. By the time we touched down at 11.30 a.m. there were very few people at the airport - the airport staff mainly- since a scheduled domestic flight had taken off only half an hour earlier, and no other scheduled flight was expected until morning of the following day.

We taxied to a spot some distance from the airport building. Olaf Olsen was waiting for us in a black bullet proof car very close to where the Cessna stopped. As soon as the propellers of the Cessna had stopped, Olsen entered the aircraft and helped carry one of the packages of the treasure. I carried the other package and followed close behind him to the car. In less than five minutes Olsen and I were on our way.

The landscape around Kiruna is one of bare undulating hills. Because of the intense cold during winter in these parts which are north of the Arctic circle, the vegetation is one of stunted trees and grass. I was to learn later that even potatoes cannot be grown in these areas since the ground is frozen for longer periods than is allowable for potatoes to mature. From a distance Olsen showed me a range of hills below which, he said, was the greatest iron ore mine in Europe. He said that at the moment the ore was being mined several hundred metres below sea level.

As we passed through the bare landscape I could see herds of reindeer with their branched horns. We drove on until we came to the edge of a longitudinal lake of brackish water, and as we approached the national park I noticed that the stunted trees gave way to treeless moors. Farther ahead there were birch forests, and on the distant mountain top I could see some snow even though it was not yet winter. Had it not been for the risks that lay ahead on this mission, my visit to this place would have been most enjoyable. To see this grandiose landscape bathed in Arctic light would have been the culmination of a life's dream. But now this perilous mission! It robbed me of all the excitement nature had spread before me.

Olsen kept glancing at his watch. We had plenty of time in hand; so he adjusted his speed so that we would not enter the national park too early or too late. The road became narrower and narrower and the surface more bumpy. At one point Olsen slowed down the car and brought it to a stop. He pointed to the edge of a birch forest about a kilometre away and said, "That's where the entrance into the park is, and that's where I will wait for you."

"Half a kilometer inside the park," I corrected.

"Yeah, O.K."

As my heart began to race and pound against my ribs, the words of Psalm 121 rose to my mind, "*The Lord shall preserve thy going out and coming in from this time forth, and even for evermore.*" Yes, although I had surrendered myself into the loving care of the Lord, and perhaps there was no need to recite to him any specific formula, I still felt Psalm 121 to be my indispensable companion; after all, theologians writing on prayer, including Father Maloney, my most favourite theologian, agree that even with contemplative prayer, certain words, phrases or statements can always form useful points of departure for wordless contemplative prayer.

Presently we arrived at the gate, the entrance into Abisko National Park. Olsen continued for another half kilometer inside the national park, and brought the car to a stop.

I stripped myself naked, except for the tight pants I had on. I took the two packages weighing twenty kilograms in all, and placed them in a sizable canvas bag which I slung across my shoulder. I started trudging along the foot path that lay in front of me. Olsen simply said, "Good Luck," and quickly retreated into the bullet proof car.

I knew that from now on my image was between the sights of powerful telescopic rifles. I knew that I was being watched through powerful binoculars. For a fraction of a second I thought, "What if, seeing a black man in their binoculars, one of them gets the crazy idea that Wickman has tricked them, and fires? I felt my knees begin to give way. Here I was trudging along an unknown path in the land of the Lapps whose origins had long been lost in the mists of antiquity. I looked up at the distant snow covered hills and I repeated, "I will lift up mine eyes unto the hills..." I had no earthly weapon with which to defend or protect myself, but I had plenty of darts to throw to the Lord who made heaven and earth. I chose one of these and started throwing it to the Lord - the Jesus Prayer, "Lord Jesus Christ son of God have mercy on me a sinner." I kept repeating this prayer, this mantra, until I reached the log cabin which stood on the right handside of the footpath.

It was 2.05 p.m when I entered the cabin; but I couldn't see a thing inside that igloo shaped cabin, because it was so dark. I had to stand still for a while to get used to the darkness. Then suddenly a beam of light pierced the cabin; for just in front of me somebody had flung open a small window from the outside. I discovered that there was a small wooden table just below the window in front of me. I deposited the bag on the table and started to retreat. As I reached the door I heard somebody running from the back of the cabin to the door, and we met just as I was emerging from the cabin. The man was wearing a black nylon mask, and had a walkie-talkie in one hand, and an automatic revolver in the other.

"Hold it," he said tersely, waving the gun and indicating that I should re-enter the cabin. I dutifully obeyed and re-entered the cabin. This, of course, was a step I had not anticipated in the scenario I had committed to memory. He ordered me to stand close to the table on which I had placed the canvas bag, while he busied himself opening several small windows. There was now enough light in the cabin to enable me see my surroundings clearly.

From a corner of the cabin he brought to the table a delicate weighing balance, a large glass jar, and some chemicals. Next he opened the canvas bag and removed the two packages I had placed in it. First he emptied the rubies on to the weighing balance and I held my breath. 'Suppose the rubies do not weigh ten kilograms exactly? Or suppose this weighting balance is defective,' well, I kept repeating the Jesus Prayer. I saw him record the weight. It was exactly ten kilograms. But was he sure that these were rubies? I watched him pour the deep red stones into the glass jar. He then poured some liquid in the jar, and shook the jar a couple of times. Then he brought a small but very powerful torch and flashed it in the jar containing the stones. The colour that emanated from the stones in the jar was fantastic. I had never seen rubies in my life, let alone known how testing for genuine rubies was done. I was seeing these things for the first time then. The man nodded and said to me, "O.K. these are rubies. Alright." He then carefully poured out the liquid and left the shining rubies in the jar.

Next he took the second package, and with the help of a small pen knife, tore open the thick cellophane cover and removed four small bars measuring about a foot each. Again my heart started racing. "Could these four small bars weigh ten kilos?" I asked myself. But then I remembered the chemistry I studied long ago, that gold or *Aurum*, to use its scientific or Latin name, was one of the heavy metals, and so it was quite possible that the four slender bars could weigh ten kilos. In fact they did! The man had the bars weighed and their weight recorded - ten kilos! I could literary feel the tautness of my nerves easing. But was it gold that he had weighed and not some fake metal? Well, he did a little test using a liquid which looked like mercury, and he nodded in satisfaction. He was sure he had gold bars before him.

Then the most extraordinary, most unexpected thing happened. The man, who was tall and well built, stood looking at me through the slits of his nylon mask. He stretched his hand and we shook hands. He said, "Thanks for the service, Chris."

Hearing this man call me by my first name I was impelled to utter only one world, "Ah!" In a more congenial atmosphere I'd have said, "How the hell did you know my name, you bustard?!" But under the circumstances, I had to confine myself to uttering the monosyllable, "Ah!"

"When d'you leave for Tanzania?" he asked.

"Monday morning," I answered. "But how did you know my name? Who are you sir?"

"Take it easy, Chris. I can't reveal myself to you here in this remote place. But I will, someday, if you could tell me where you are staying. We will talk some more then. What we must do immediately now is to clear from this place as fast as we can; for very soon planes will be flying over this place like locusts, looking for us. Proceed now to the other cabin down hill and take Linda away. Here is the key of the padlock we've locked her with and say "Hallo" to Tom. Hope the little money I gave him helped him to get to Stockholm."

I told him we were staying at Diplomat Hotel. But all the while I was with this man I was trying to figure out who he was. I strained all my powers of recall, for something in his voice seemed to ring a bell, as if I had heard that voice before. But where? I could not remember.

There wasn't much time to waste, and the man was clearly in a hurry to get away. So he escorted me outside the cabin, and as I was half running towards the second cabin I could hear him speaking into his walkie talkie, "Everything's O.K. Don't shoot, over! I repeat, don't shoot, treasure is genuine and intact. Over!"

I hurried to the cabin below. When I entered, Linda was browsing through some old magazines strewn on the floor. She was sitting on an improvised bed of straw, but her ankle was tied with a thick iron chain secured by a heavy padlock. The chain was tied to one of the poles supporting the log cabin.

Linda stood up to give me a bear hug, but I was in no mood for that. First things first. I went to work immediately. Having located the padlock on Linda's ankle, I inserted the key given to me by the mysterious thug, and the padlock snapped open. Linda was free.

We left the cabin and started half running towards our car, following a different footpath. What with the rough times she had had in the last four days, Linda could not walk fast enough. I had half a mind of carrying her on my shoulders. On second thoughts, however, I decided not to; for, weakened though she was, Linda must have weighed at least sixty five kilos, and the idea of breaking my vertebra in this remote place north of the Arctic circle, was not particularly inviting to me.

We reached the car and Olsen started the engine as soon as we were seated in the car. I told Olsen that I'd put on my clothes when we got to Kiruna airport. For the time being my pants would do.

It took us less than two hours to get to Kiruna airport, for this time Olsen pressed the accelerator pedal really hard. Just outside the airport area we pulled by the road side, and I had time to put on my clothes and look more respectable.

I think it is worth recording here that while we were driving from Abisko to Kiruna, Linda showered me with kisses as she kept saying, "Thank you, thank you." But while I appreciated that, my thoughts were elsewhere, I was re-living Psalm 121, "*The Lord shall preserve thy going out and thy coming in from this time forth, and even for evermore!*" I could sense the reality of these words with the faith which could move mountains. Indeed, I had been preserved. I also recalled the Jesus Prayer that had never left my lips while in Abisko National Park, and was convinced that the son of God had indeed shown mercy on me, a sinner! In thanksgiving for what had happened, I silently recited the *magnificat*, ... "for he has done great things to me and holy is his name...." Like a butterfly hovering from flower to flower, I found myself again mumbling this and that prayer of thanksgiving; in other words, indulging in discursive prayer, until I once again remembered Father George Maloney's insistent advice, "Rather than indulge in discursive prayer, the best thing we can do is to surrender ourselves totally to that intimacy with the Lord to which he calls us..." With that sublime thought in my mind, I made an effort to lose myself in a contemplative milieu.

Olsen steered the car to where Mr. Wickman had parked the Cessna. Linda left the car and ran into the outstretched arms of her father. Wickman shed tears of joy as he embraced his daughter. Then he turned towards me and repeated the bear hug he had given to his daughter. I could see that he was overcome with emotion as he embraced me and kept repeating, "Thank you, thank you for everything."

At one end of the run way I could see a number of helicopters. These, I was told, were police helicopters which had been lined up to fly to Abisko National Park to try to capture the terrorists. I considered this to be a futile exercise; for already two hours had elapsed since we left the park and if, as the mysterious terrorist who knew my first name had said, they intended to clear off from that cursed hideout of theirs at the earliest, it was quite clear to me that by now they had either already mingled themselves with the inhabitants of the small lake side town of Abisko farther to the north, or driven as far away as Norway if they fancied doing so. Also, exactly how armed policemen flying in helicopters were going to capture terrorists hiding in a national park was beyond my ability to comprehend. In any case, this latest development about the state's intervention in this affair by the use of helicopters and policemen, did not originate from Mr. Wickman.

Mr. Wickman helped his daughter on to the Cessna and showed me my seat, and we taxied off, leaving Olaf Olsen to start the long drive back to Stockholm, and the armed policemen to embark on their fruitless adventure.

9

It took us only an hour to fly from Kiruna to Lulea. At Lulea airport Mr. Wickman rang the castle, and after about fifteen minutes a huge cream coloured Mercedes benz arrived and we were driven to the castle.

Entering the precincts of the castle one could understand why owners of such places could easily become the targets of machinations by the less fortunate members of society. Every aspect of this place spoke of opulence. I did not envy the Wickmans for their immense wealth, because it seemed to me that such people had only two alternatives to choose from: either to get reconciled to the idea that they were museum pieces and therefore to make absolutely sure that they kept indoors all the time, or to do everything in their power to display their opulence to the general public, in which case the possibility of their being abducted at gun point was never far away.

We entered the castle, and it was all joy and merriment as Linda's mother and the castle staff mobbed Linda and myself to give Linda a fitting welcome home, and me a hero's welcome. The merriment was marred by one thing only: the longest serving valet was missing. I overheard one of the assistants tell Mr. Wickman that the valet, Gregesen, had left a note in his room saying that he had received a telegram from Copenhagen informing him of the death of his mother and that he had left in a hurry, driving the old Renault to the southern town of Malmo from where he would take a boat to Copenhagen. However he had promised to be back some time later.

That same evening the Wickmans and their family lawyer met in a secret meeting to which I was not invited. But it transpired at that meeting, so I was informed by Linda afterwards, that the question of rewarding me for the service I had rendered was discussed. The reward was revealed to me by Mr. Wickman the following morning. Its details must, of course, remain a guarded secret, at the moment, but what I can say here is that if you ever heard the song which talks of the chap who rose from a jack to a king, that chap could have been me!

Arrangements were made for me to catch the afternoon plane to Stockholm so as to be in time for the Minister's reception that evening.

* * * * *

The first thing I did when I got into my room in Diplomat Hotel was to ring Tom.

"Hallo," I called.

"Hallo," Tom answered. "You are back?"

"Yeah, indeed I am. This is not a ghost like yours the other day. This is me."

"Successful?"

"Yes, with God's help."

"Good gracious! You know what Chris, I am not used to praying. But this time I had to. When you rang just now I was actually kneeling in prayer. I was mumbling something to the effect that you should get back in one piece."

"So I am in one piece, alright; or if you like, whole and entire."

"Tell me, Chris, what's it really that prayer does? Does prayer influence God's decision? I mean, can you change God's decision by praying?"

"Tom, you are asking me a very serious question. It would require a whole lecture to expound on this issue. The only satisfactory theological treaties on prayer I have read is one by C. S. Lewis. No, I would not put it as crudely as you have put it, that prayer influences the decision of the omniscient God. Rather, prayer influences you. It influences your faith in God; and it is faith which works wonders."

"Would you say, for instance, that the prayer I have just been saying for you has been answered, now that you are, as I wished you to be, whole and entire, when in fact the events took place yesterday?"

"Tom, do you ever read theological writings? These problems are adequately expounded by theologians. You see, theologians, like Father Maloney S. J. talk about "God's everlasting now'. You and me are accustomed to thinking in terms of the space-time continuum. With God there is no past, present and future. God does not exist in a space-time continuum. He exists in the everlasting now moment! So the prayer you said for me was foreseen by God in his everlasting now moment even before you left Dar es

Salaam, or before you were born, for that matter!"

"Chris, you boggle my mind with your theological explanations. When we get back to Dar es Salaam you should lend me some of your books so I can read about these things. For the moment I'm dying to see you. Why don't you nip off to my room so you can tell me everything?"

"I'll take a shower and come over soon after. By the way, what time's the reception?"

"Starts at 7p.m. Somebody will pick us up from here."

"Do people know anything about my adventures? I mean those who will be at the party? I would hate to be mobbed and asked questions."

"None whatsoever other than myself. Not a word has appeared in the papers. I think it's to our credit that this operation was executed absolutely marvelously. I mean the Wickmans, the Central bank president, Olsen and ourselves did well to keep our lips tight. Hurry up, I'm dying to see you."

I took a shower and put on my best suit knowing that from Tom's room we would move straight to the party. I refrained from ringing David fearing that if I did, it would be impossible for me to be left alone with Tom.

Tom almost crushed my ribs when he hugged me the moment I stepped inside his room.

"Boy," he said, "how did you do it? Did the thugs threaten to kill you? How was Linda when you found her?"

He must have asked at least five questions at a stretch without waiting for an answer.

I then slowly went through the story of my adventure from the time I left the bullet proof car at the end of the road inside Abisko National Park to the time I climbed into Mr. Wickman's Cessna for our flight to Lulea.

Tom was all attention while I was narrating the story. He was particularly intrigued to hear that the thug addressed me by my first name, and that it was the same thug who had given Tom some money for his fare to Stockholm.

"You say he called you by your first name?" Tom asked incredulously.

"Yes, I was surprised beyond measure."

"And he said he was the one who gave me the money?"

"Yes."

"And he said you should say "Hallo" to me?"

"That's exactly what he said."

"Couldn't you tell who he was from his voice?"

"The voice seemed to ring a bell in my mind, but with that black nylon mask over his head and face, it was simply impossible to know who he was."

"He must be somebody who knows us intimately," observed Tom. " He may have worked in Tanzania. Can't you recall some of your former staff at ILD? Can't you remember one whose stature resembled that of the man you saw?"

"Wait a minute, Tom. Now that you say it, I'm beginning to recall to mind all the Swedish staff we had at ILD. That man could have been Hanson, Gustav Hanson. Among the Swedish staff we had, Hanson was the only one of that stature. You remember Hanson who was in Professor Meffert's team? I used to invite him to the Board meetings whenever we discussed examination results, since he was our Examinations Officer. It's surprising why I couldn't remember his voice. Although I cannot say I am hundred percent sure it was him, I bet it was Hanson!"

"Yes, the man who gave me money at that lonely spot was the size of Hanson who used to attend our meetings at ILD," Tom agreed.

"The more I think of him the more I am convinced it was Gustav Hanson," I said.

"Did you say he said he would visit you one of these days?"

"Yes, that's what he said!"

"O.K., then, in that case we don't need to wreck our heads figuring out who this man is. He will show up someday. But, Chris, my stand is this: whoever he is, let's not cause any trouble here. It will not help us if we betray him to the authorities. Linda's been found. No blood has been shed. Let us leave this country as peacefully as we got in. By the way, Chris, how did Wickman reward you?"

I hesitated a bit, but since Tom had confided his secrets to me I thought it unfair to withhold mine from him. So I told him briefly how I had risen from a jack to a king, and we shook hands.

"Keep it to yourself," was all that Tom said.

I assured him that I would keep my secret and his, to myself. Tom put on a white *kanzu*, black jacket, sandals, and an expensive *barkashia*. He looked very much like an Imam about to enter a mosque to lead prayers. We were ready for the Minister's reception.

David was waiting for Tom in the hotel lobby. When he saw me, surprise registered over his face, he moved to greet me and said, "I have been looking for you since yesterday morning. Where've you been?"

"Sorry, I didn't tell you David, but I had to sneak away to meet somebody. But here I am alright."

David was not the kind of person who delighted in meddling in other people's affairs. So he simply let the matter pass.

Mr. Chale from the Tanzania Embassy drove us to the Minister's residence. What impressed me upon seeing the Minister's residence was the simplicity of the place. Whereas our Ministers at home live in palatial buildings, this residence by comparison, was quite unassuming. It was a one storey building with combined sitting room - dinning room, a kitchen and a few other rooms on the ground floor, and a few more rooms, probably bedrooms, on the top floor.

The party was being held in the small garden behind the house. There were about thirty people at the party, most of whom being the staff of the Tanzania embassy and other African embassies. But there was a sprinkling of white guests too, mostly from SIDA and the Ministry of Lands and Environment.

It was while we were chatting and moving round the soft turf with glasses in our hands, that I noticed somebody talking to Minister Msokonde and Tom. I approached the little group, and to my great astonishment I found myself face to face with Gustav Hanson.

"Hi, Chris," Hanson said, gripping my hand in a warm handshake. He was dressed in a smart grey suit, and no stretch of the imagination could associate this gentleman with terrorists who go about adducting millionaire's daughters.

"Hi, Gustav," I answered. "What a small world. Who could've thought we would meet again here in Sweden? When you last wrote me the address was of a German town."

"Yeah, as I told you, I worked for some time with Professor Meffert at the University of Gottingen. But late last year I rejoined my old institute in Goteborg."

"Had I known that, I'd have written to you in advance, so we could've arranged to visit your institute."

"Oh, even now you're welcome. When d'you leave?"

"Monday morning. We don't have much time left to travel to Goteborg. Let's hope we get another chance next time. Hey, Gustav, how did you know about this reception?"

" Well, you see, Mr. Jacobson the Minister, happens to come from my county. He is in fact my Member of Parliament, and a former collegemate of mine. I dropped in at his office this morning to say 'hallo' to him and he thought it a good idea that I should come to the party to meet Tanzanian friends. I knew that you and the permanent Secretary would be present, so I made sure I'd come along."

Gustav and I were talking loudly enough for anybody near us to hear. Then Gustav moved a few steps in the direction of the drinks table to refill his glass. But before moving away he made a slight movement of his head suggesting that I should follow him. I took the cue; and since it was so natural to move from place to place on the soft turf, nobody could suspect that Gustav and I were about to engage in the uncovering of a secret.

As soon as we were at a safe distance from anybody else, Gustav remarked between long draughts of his drink, "Hey, Chris, how did you like it up there?"

"How d'you mean, up there?"

He laughed, and moving closer to me, he whispered in my ear, "Up there in the log cabin in Abisko!" Then putting his finger across his lips he said, "sh, sh, sh! don't breathe a word. I've a pleasant surprise for you - your reward for the service you did us. I'll be seeing you tomorrow at your hotel and I'll tell you more about it. But let's agree on the time."

"Will ten o'clock suit you?" I asked. "I know that by then everyone of us will be out shopping or doing something else."

I was so jolted by Hanson's revelation that I almost spilled my drink. So it was Gustav Hanson with his gang who had abducted Linda Wickman! It was Gustav who had given Tom money for his fare. It was Gustav who mentioned my name in that far off sport on the fringes of God's earth! I found it hard to believe that I could not recognize the voice of a person I had lived with at ILD for over two years. It is surprising to what extent a nylon mask or hood can disguise a person's physical appearance, and since psychologically we tend to associate a person's voice with his physical features, when the latter are disguised the voice also seems to change.

Drinks flowed freely at this party: whisky, brandy, gin, beer: they were all there for people to choose. Delicious bites were also plentiful: prawns, fish eggs on toast, and lobster; even the dark looking reindeer meat with its rather pungent smell was there. Flat fish, which is a special Swedish delicacy was also being served.

People were already talking spiritedly and one could hear laughter emanating from every corner of the garden especially laughter made by the wives and daughters of the Tanzanian embassy staff and Tanzanian students.

I located David surrounded by a group of Tanzanian girls. It was he who was the source of the laughter that was emanating from the group. He was already stoned and was therefore cracking dirty jokes. In all fairness to him, however, I must say David had behaved remarkably well during our sojourn in Sweden so far. Each evening he had been taking a beer or two at dinner time, and that was all. But this evening, seeing that all official engagements were over and as if he meant to compensate for the sacrifice he had made during the week, he drank like one who was bent on punishing the bottles. He was changing from beer to whisky, to wine, to gin and tonic, and back to beer.

It was this strange mixture of alcoholic beverages that not only gave rise to the inane conversation that caused so much laughter among the girls, but also made David vomit. Fortunately only the Tanzanian girls saw him vomit, and when the uncontrollable antiperistaltic movement began, he had the good sense of turning his face to the mulberry hedge of the garden.

Joyce Mhina, daughter of Ambassador Mhina saw what was happening, so like the sensible girl she was, she moved quickly and stood behind David, thus obstructing the light and leaving David in semidarkness. None of the dignitaries at the party knew what had happened, but Joyce reckoned it was wise to avert embarrassment in case there was a recurrence of the antiperistatic movement in David's bowels. So she approached me and whispered to me about what had happened, and suggested that I take David back to the hotel. I whispered to Mr. Chale, and he obliged by agreeing to take us back to the hotel.

I got hold of David's arm and simply dragged him out of the compound amidst his curses and protestations to the effect that it was against human rights to interfere with somebody's freedom to enjoy himself. I did not speak a word, of course, bearing in mind, as the joke goes, that if you argue with a drunkard, people might not notice the difference between the two of you. With my iron grip round his upper arm, I made quite sure he followed my steps to Mr. Chale's car. It took us only seven minutes to reach Diplomat Hotel. I dragged David out of the car, and said goodbye to Mr. Chale who was returning to the party to join Tom and the others.

"Now, steady David," I said. "I don't want you to draw people's attention by slumping to the ground in a heap. Pull yourself together until we get to your room."

While I was getting our room keys from the reception desk, the girl at the counter looked at me giggling, "Your friend had a drop too many?" she asked.

"Some of your Swedish drinks are too strong for us," I teased.

"Tell him to lock his door, to switch off the lights, and not to leave a lighted cigarette while he is asleep, it might cause a fire," the girl insisted.

"Don't worry Miss, I know exactly what I'll do. I'll switch off the lights after he's gone to bed, and then I'll lock him in."

The young receptionist laughed thinking I was joking. But that's exactly what I did. I left the lights in the toilet so he could see his way, but otherwise I switched off the other lights, locked the door and took the key away.

Early the next morning I tip-toed to David's room and unlocked the door. David was still in bed snoring noisily. Instead of waking him up I quietly removed the sheets he was covered with and with my hand explored the bed to see if all was well; for my worst fear had been that he might wet the bed. Fortunately David had flung himself into bed with his suit on. He had only managed to remove his shoes and loosen his tie. So, while the trousers were definitely soiled, the clean white sheets were more or less spared. More or less, I say, because there was slight wetness somewhere on one of the sheets, which I hoped, the woman making the beds on our floor would not notice.

Being disgusted as I was, I saw no reason why I should treat him gently. So I gave him a rather violent shake, and he woke up.

"David," I called, "You've put us all to shame."

"Why?"

"You vomited at the party yesterday; and look at what you've done to your trousers."

"Never mind my trousers. But did you say I vomited at the party?"

"Yes, you did."

"Did people see me vomit? I mean, could anyone swear in a court of law that he saw me vomit?"

I felt that indulging in a conversation of such inanity was not my idea of passing time.

So I decided to leave him for the moment and return to my room to get ready for breakfast. As I was moving towards the door David pleaded with me, "Please," he said, " are you sure my head isn't floating away?"

"How d'you mean, floating away?"

"I mean isn't it coming off its moorings and leaving the stump alone? It's throbbing so hard, I fear unless you do something, I may lose my head."

"Okay, I'll bring you some aspirin tablets."

"No, not aspirin. Bring me a glass of cold milk. That'll do the trick."

"Right, I'll bring you a glass of cold milk and some aspirin. Meanwhile, you take a cold shower, will you?"

I left David's room wondering why otherwise intelligent and highly read people can bring themselves to such low levels of behaviour. Inwardly however, I was grateful that this shameful thing hadn't been noticed by people other than the few Tanzanian girls and Mr. Chale. But what pleased me more was the knowledge that our Minister, Peter Msokonde, was at this very moment, namely, seven o'clock Saturday morning, catching his plane at Stockholm airport. He wasn't going to be at breakfast to ask possible embarrassing questions, in case one of the girls had leaked a word to him. Tom was also not likely to be with me at breakfast as he had escorted the Minister to the airport.

I had breakfast alone and returned to David's room. After I had satisfied myself that David had taken a shower, changed his clothes and generally tidied up himself, I rang for room service and asked for a continental breakfast, plus a glass of cold milk to be brought to David's room. For a person nursing a heavy hang over, an English breakfast of fried eggs and bacon is the last thing he wants to see. But a continental one of corn flakes, passion fruit or lemon juice, dry French bread, marmalade and black coffee, is easily tolerated.

Before David's breakfast was brought I forced him to swallow two aspirin tables. After he had his breakfast he seemed to get back to normal rather fast. It was clear to me that he was used to these hangovers. I left his room without telling him how I intended to spend that Saturday and the next day; and David did not tell me how he was going to spend the two days. All we knew was that we were scheduled to depart at nine o'clock the following Monday.

10

I returned to my room in Diplomat Hotel intending to continue reading an interesting Chapter from Father George A. Maloney's book entitled *Out of the Body Experiences*. Father Maloney claims that there is overwhelming evidence in support of the reality of life after death. He says that interviews with thousands of people from different parts of the world who have had near death experience indicate that these people experienced a transcendence, a lifting up into a foreign region or dimension of great light and beauty.... They often meet apparitions of the dead, or some guide who is a being of light.

I had hardly finished reading half of this enthralling chapter when the telephone in my room rang. It was ten o'clock then, and the girl at the reception desk told me that a certain Mr. Gustav Hanson was waiting for me in the hotel lobby. He didn't want to come to my room but preferred to see me in the lobby if I didn't mind.

I locked my room and quickly descended the flight of steps to the reception desk, and on to the lobby of the hotel. Hanson was sitting in one of the soft sofa seats, puffing a huge cuban cigar. He heaved himself up from the sofa to greet me, and I sat in another seat facing his.

"You left the party rather unceremoniously yesterday, didn't you?" Hanson asked.

"I had to, to divert disaster."

"Yeah, I could see that your friend was quite tight. I saw you drag him away and I thought it was wise of you to do that. Now Chris, I suggest we move from here to a more congenial place where we can talk."

Without wasting time we left the elegant Diplomat Hotel, hailed a taxi, and after some minutes we found ourselves in a shabby crowded pub somewhere. I could not understand how a person of Hanson's intelligence could regard this run down joint as a more congenial place. But remembering the Lulea and Abisko episodes I could appreciate why Hanson and his gang had to prefer joints like this at least for a time while the dust settled.

Hanson led me to a table in a corner of the pub where the light was rather subdued. He ordered some drinks, but I declined to take any alcoholic drink after the previous night's carousing, and preferred only fruit juice. To my surprise, I saw Hanson beginning to work on some hard stuff at this hour of the day.

"Now Chris, I want first to introduce my colleagues to you," Hanson said.

He left the table and lost himself among the patrons who were doing all sorts of things: drinking, smoking illicit joints, playing darts and gambling. Presently he returned accompanied by three chaps, two of whom were well known to me. These were Peter Lindberg and Goran Frisk. Peter, Goran and Gustav Hanson had all been in professor Meffert's team at my institute, and as I have already recorded earlier, the UNDP team of experts had left our institute two years ago. But whereas professor Meffert was back in his home country, Germany, and professor Samwelson had returned to his former job at the University of Upsalla, and Hanson had rejoined his former institute in Goteborg, I wasn't sure what the others were doing.

Both Peter and Goran shook hands with me

"Hi, Mr. Principal," Peter Lindberg said, "how are my friends in Dar?" Most of the younger expatriate staff at ILD used to address me as 'Mr. Principal' even though I objected to it. Only the older members like Professors Meffert and Samwelson and the Land Surveyor Gustav Hanson would call me by my first name.

"Your friends at ILD are fine," I said. "But I'm not so sure about the others in the bars and night clubs of Dar," I joked.

"You would not know them, anyway; especially those at the Tours and Hungers in Ubungo. Remember I said at the farewell party at Agip Motel, that I would return to Dar someday to look for my girlfriends?" Lindberg asked.

"Of course, I do."

"Well, I meant those at Tours and Hunters night club," Lindberg said.

Hanson said, "I think you three had better continue playing darts while I talk to Chris. If we all sit round this table and begin to talk people might begin to suspect we're up to something."

Lindberg, Goran and the other chap left and joined the other patrons at the darts board. As soon as they had left, Hanson began, "Chris, we want to thank you for the service you did us, even if unwittingly. We've agreed to buy you a Landrover which will be shipped to you next week. Knowing the roads in Mbinga district, we thought a Landrover was the best choice."

As he was speaking, I was already trembling inwardly. My conscience reproached me in no uncertain manner, 'You can't accept this ill gotten present! But I must confess I had no guts to make my stand known. I kept quiet. But keeping quiet really meant tacit acceptance of the present. The tacit acceptance of the present already made me feel the pangs of remorse and shame. However, I continued listening to Hanson.

"Chris," Hanson continued, "I want to tell you a little more about this affair; for I know you must be feeling disappointed by the behaviour of your former staff members. The three of us are the ones who pulled off Linda's abduction and the subsequent windfall in the form of the ransom treasure you brought us."

I interrupted, "You mean Lindberg and Goran were also involved in this thing?"

"That's precisely what I'm saying. The three of us did it."

"But why did you did it, Gustav?"

"I'll tell you. You see, before we joined the ILD, in fact even before we joined the UNDP, all the three of us were working in Wickman's company: I as a Land Surveyor, Goran and Linberg as mining engineers. It was the three of us who opened the gold mines at Lukalasi and Mpepo. I prepared the cadastral and geological maps while my colleagues directed the mining engineering.

In the first two years of operation we hit upon a gold bearing reef which was so rich that Wickman became the third richest man in Europe. The following year Wickman acquired mining rights in the Morogoro and Ulanga areas. There again, we discovered a lot of rubies. In all those years Mr. Tom Nyirenda was the Commissioner for Minerals in the then Ministry of Energy and Minerals." Hanson stopped for a while to swallow the hard stuff he was drinking.

"As I was saying," he continued, "all those three or four years, Nyirenda was the man who mattered in that Ministry. Both the Minister and the Permanent Secretary were only figure heads. Nyirenda was the man who could direct you where to go for prospecting if you were to have any luck. But more importantly, Nyirenda happened to have some old but very detailed topographical and geological maps drawn by the Germans at the turn of the century. These maps show in detail places of mineral occurrence. Of course, Nyirenda did not make these maps available to everybody, but Wickman was able to strike a deal with him, that if through the use of these maps he, Wickman, could discover rich gold deposits, he would repay Nyirenda in kind. In fact he offered to make him a partner in the company."

Hanson took one long draught of his drink, and poured some more in the glass. He continued, "It was through the use of these maps that we were able to start a mine at Lukalasi and later at Mpepo. You see, when you are equipped with good topographical and geological maps your work as a prospector is made that much easier. You don't simply rely on trial and error, and as you know, in those days we didn't have the kind of sophisticated prospecting equipment they have today. So it was important to have at least good reliable maps."

I interrupted. "It was very fortunate that you started those two mines in Mbinga district. They have offered employment to our people in the district."

"Of course, yes, although Mbinga is not a poor district. People could be gainfully employed in their coffee shambas even if no gold had been discovered. Still, I guess, the two mines have added to the economic progress of the district."

"Oh, they definitely have," I said. "But, mind you, not everybody in Mbinga district grows coffee. For example, my own people living on the shores of lake Nyasa have hardly any worth-while economic activity. Most of our young men have flocked to the mines."

"Now Chris," Hanson said, "you may be wondering how we fell foul of Mr. Wickman."

"I was about to ask that."

"Well, you see, it was I who did the negotiations with Tom Nyirenda about the German maps. I'm the one who blazed the trail in the bush, in order to prepare larger maps on the basis of the worn out German maps. My two colleagues and I reached an agreement with Wickman that we would be shareholders in the Company. Of course he had the majority of the shares. He was, to all intents and purposes, the real owner of the mines. We were only small share holders. But the way he treated us!"

At this point I saw Hanson gnashing his teeth and with folded fists he banged the table, and his otherwise serene countenance changed, and he became furious. "The way he treated us, that bastard!" He shouted. "You know what he did to us?" He asked rhetorically. "He bought our shares and threw us out of the company."

"Why did he do that?" I asked.

"For a little mistake one of us made, which really had nothing to do with our professional competence."

"Why didn't you object, or sue him?"

"We tried to institute legal proceedings through our lawyers. But you know how protracted and costly legal proceedings can be. In the end we had to give up and withdraw the case."

"Do you feel now that you've had your revenge?"

"We've at least claimed some of our sweat back."

We moved to another corner of the pub where we were once again joined by Goran and Lindberg. It was about twelve noon then and we had some snacks and beer together. Our conversation then, was of a general nature only, and it was centred on reminiscences of old days at ILD.

Hanson suggested that it was time we broke up the gathering. I understood his point. These people were on the run. The intelligence service was busy trying to identify the terrorists who had caused so much stir in the last few days. Knowing the background story that Hanson had just unfolded to me, it was not far fetched to imagine Mr. Wickman tipping the intelligence service about people like Hanson, Goran and Lindberg, people who had a grudge against him.

Hanson hailed a taxi for me, and instructed the driver to take me to Diplomat hotel. Before saying goodbye to the group, I asked for Hanson's address, which he willingly gave me.

I returned to my room in the hotel quietly, not wishing either Tom or David to know that I had returned. In any case, I wasn't even sure that they were in the hotel. This being a Saturday, we were all left to our own devices. For instance, what could have prevented Tom from visiting his villa, even though it had been leased to a law firm? Or what could have prevented David from visiting his old buddies after he had shaken off the hang over?

As usual, I threw myself into bed, only to find myself being tormented inwardly. "Yes," I thought, "a Landrover may be the best choice for the terrain in Mbinga as Hanson had put it, but was it right to accept such a present?" My conscience was gnawing inside me, loud and clear, "You should never accept this present. To accept it is to accept ill-gotten goods."

According to Hanson the Landrover was being offered to me as a token of thanks for service rendered. But I asked myself, "What service had I rendered?" The answer came, "I had brought Hanson and his gang treasure robbed from Wickman." Then I thought of the reward that had made me rise from a jack to a king. Was there any difference between Wickman's present to me and Hanson's? Wickman had rewarded me for a good service rendered to him. What service? The service of risking my life to save his daughter.'

The truth flashed into my mind as clear as a flash of lightning. It was as if I was hearing a locution which said, 'Whereas the latter is a legitimate reward, the former is not."

At this point the words of Psalm 121 drifted into my consciousness. "He shall preserve thee from hence forth and even for evermore." I also recalled the *Magnificat* I had recited when leaving the forbidding environment of Abisko National Park, "He has filled the hungry with good things, the rich he has sent away empty handed….." I was indeed a jack, but hadn't I become a king in my own small way? If I allowed myself to be the proud owner of a brand new Landrover acquired under dubious circumstances, who could tell if one day I might not be sent away empty handed?

I realized then that I was passing through the phases of a temptation, as the theologians put it: fist the encounter with the temptation as it presents itself to my consciousness. I reached this stage when Hanson first made his proposition about the Landrover. Then comes the internal debate whether or not to accept the proposition. Next comes the decision to accept or reject it; and finally the actual execution of the act of accepting or rejecting the proposition.

I reached the point of actually refusing Hanson's proposition when I got up from bed and penned a few lines which I dropped into the post office box just outside the hotel. This is what I wrote:

"Dear Hanson,
You were right when you said that a Landrover is the best choice for the roads in Mbinga. But considering the circumstances, I feel conscience bound to decline the offer.
To ensure that you do not proceed with execution of plan, I am hereby making this solemn promise to you: I shall not betray you to the authorities if you do not execute the plan. But if you do ship the cursed thing to me, I shall use all available diplomatic channels to expose you to the authorities. I hate to think that if perchance you were to be thus exposed, you would remain a hunted man at least in the eyes of Martin Wickman.

Regards,
Chris".

I folded the little missive and placed it in one of the hotel envelopes kindly provided by the hotel management. I left my room, bought a stamp at the reception counter and walked a few steps on the pavement outside, and posted the letter to Hanson using the address he had given me. I knew that the letter would reach him at the earliest by Monday, if he returned to Goteborg that Saturday. By the time he read it, I would be in mid-flight to our blessed motherland, Tanzania.

As I had expected, neither Tom nor David was in the hotel that afternoon, for after I had posted my letter to Hanson, I noticed the keys to their rooms in the pigeon holes at the reception desk. They hadn't returned by dinner time, and I had to dine alone.

However, I was relieved to see Tom at breakfast the following morning, but David was nowhere to be seen.

"Where were you yesterday, Tom? I was worried there might've been a repeat of last week's event," I said.

"Nothing of the sort. I went to my villa to tie up a few loose ends," Tom answered. Tom and I spent most of the Sunday morning visiting Tanzanian friends to bid them farewell and take their small parcels for their loved ones at home. We returned to the hotel by mid- day, but still David hadn't returned and I became worried, fearing that he might have been found drunk in the street on Saturday night, and been picked up by the city police.

Soon after breakfast on Monday, Tom and I settled our hotel bills and formally checked out of the hotel, ready to be taken to the airport. The key to David's room could still be seen in the pigeon hole, so I enquired about David from the receptionist at the counter. I was told that David had settled his hotel bill and checked out of the hotel at eleven o'clock the previous day. That was about the time I was chatting with Hanson and his colleagues in the pub.

I was horrified to say the least. How could one explain such strange behaviour? You come to a foreign country and allow yourself to be stoned because you can't control your drinking. Then when a friend administers to you a life restoring pick-me-up in the form of cold fresh milk, you quietly dissolve into thin air without leaving a trace of your whereabouts. I found this behaviour as revolting as it was inexplicable.

Tom was more philosophical than myself. He was always cool headed in times of crises. He said to me, "Look here Chris, David is not a small boy. He is, in fact, the oldest among us. He must know what he is doing. If he had disappeared leaving his luggage in the hotel and without settling his bill, we might have cause for worry. But seeing that he settled his bill properly and took his luggage with him, I bet he must have planned what he did. I bet too that we may meet him at the airport."

There was a lot of sense in what Tom had said, so without giving David another thought we left for the airport.

Our delegation had traveled first class from Dar to Stockholm, and we were now returning as first class passengers. So after the departure formalities were over, Tom and I entered the VIP departure lounge to await the final call for boarding. I had a faint hope that I might spot David in the departure lounge, but he was nowhere to be seen.

Boarding time came and passengers began to hurry across the tarmac to the huge Scandinavian aircraft parked near by. It was then that I spotted David hurrying to the aircraft. Walking by his side was an African lady dressed in a beautifully tailored Kitenge dress and a leather coat.

David had also spotted me. He held the lady by the hand and both of them moved quickly towards me. He touched my shoulder and said "Mr. Principal, you didn't mean to leave me behind in Sweden, did you?"

I looked at him almost wishing to slap him in the face. I said, "Really, David, you almost gave me a heart attack. I was worried sick about you."

"You needn't have worried about me, Chris, look what I've got," he whispered." This is Tsala Chambakare, my wife," he said pointing his hand to the lady standing close by.

"Your what?" I asked, stretching my hand to shake hands with her.

"My wife," he repeated. "My long lost wife; the one I told you in Dar had eloped with one of the ruling party leaders. I will tell you the full story when we get back to Dar."

11

Tom was summoned to the Chief Secretary's Office a week after our return from Sweden. The aging Chief Secretary, Mr. Oswald Mkangama, was usually good natured and fatherly when it came to disciplining senior civil servants like Permanent Secretaries. At this time, he had only a few months to retire, so he was in no mood to throw his weight about. Looking forward to an honorable and well deserved retirement, he was not about to create enemies at a time when he most needed friends.

The old man showed Tom a chair and began at once, "What's this I hear about you, Tom? Msokonde has been to see the President and he has said nasty things about you."

"What has he said?" Tom asked.

"That while in Sweden you kept falling out of the group; that you were always in the company of strange women. It's pointless to deny these allegations because Msokonde brought to the President a copy of one of the Swedish papers, and we had a person from the Swedish Embassy here to translate the article for us. The story is indeed true, and if I may add, revolting too. Msokonde is urging that you be removed from the Ministry."

"Yes, sir," Tom answered, "the story is true, that a Swedish friend of mine and myself got abducted by some thugs. But they were after the Swedish friend, not me. That's why they released me after a few minutes."

Tom went on to tell Mr. Mkangama the full story. He knew Mkangama very well. He knew his weakness too. Especially now that he was soon retiring, Tom knew that Mkangama was eager to ensure that his future was not going to be miserable. So he told him everything regarding his relationship with Wickman. He ended by making a rather strange proposal to the Chief Secretary.

"Sir, if you will listen to me carefully, I'd like to make the following proposal. If, as you say, Msokonde wants me removed, I suggest you advise the President to send me back to the Ministry of Energy and Minerals; and to make it clear that I've been demoted, to send me there not as Permanent Secretary but as Commissioner for Minerals, my former position. This will no doubt please Msokonde. But let me assure you, sir, that if you do that, you will personally gain immensely. In that position, I'll ensure you become a senior partner in one of Wickman's companies. With a retired Chief Secretary sitting on one of his Company Boards, I'm sure Wickman will feel proud. I'll see to it that you do sit on one of those Boards. You see, your job will simply be to attend occasional Board Meetings; but the remuneration! You will remember me throughout your life, old man."

Tom had made his point. Mr. Mkangama's eyes began to sparkle. He said, "Tom you've always been good to me. Between us, and between these four walls, I've never liked that haughty young man, your Minister. So, after he had antagonized the President against you, I saw the President and persuaded him from taking action, at least until we had heard your side of the story. He agreed that I should talk to you first. Now after what you've just told me, I'm going to suggest to him that we do just as you've proposed. All these days I've been thinking how I'm going to spend my retirement; and as you know, the pension is so meagre, it is not worth even thinking about."

"Do as I've suggested, Sir, and I'll take care of you," Tom said after the Chief Secretary had finished speaking.

"But I've something else to tell you, Sir," Tom continued. "As this is a showdown between me and Msokone, I think I'd be failing in my duty if I withhold from you certain vital information about him."

The fatherly looking Chief Secretary leaned forward to listen to what Tom had to say.

Tom unzipped the small leather brief case he had brought with him and took out a stack of complementary slips written to him by Minister Msokonde on different occasions. He placed them in front of Mr. Mkangama and said, "Sir, look at these; and if you care to read them you'll know what kind of person your Minister is. I've been inundated by these things ever since I started working with this man."

While Tom was speaking, the Chief Secretary was perusing the complementary slips one by one. One slip said, "Ensure he gets the plot. He's my close friend...." Another said, "Don't mind what they say about double allocation. Give him the plot and we can advise the President to revoke the other man's title...." A more serious one said, "What are the technicalities of selling an island to an individual? Please advise. Would like to sell Ngindo Island in Lake Nyasa to Mr. Van Meer of Johannesburg."

As the Chief Secretary continued perusing slip after slip he kept shaking his head. Then he looked up at Tom and said, "Why didn't you let us know about this earlier? So all the noise the MPs make in Parliament about these things, is in fact genuine?"

"Oh yes, it is quite genuine. All their complaints are true," Tom said, "although of course, I've tried my best to resist entertaining these requests."

At this juncture Tom fished out from his brief case a folded page he had removed from a file. It was the question sent to his Ministry by Mr. Shedrick Yalomba, MP for Unyanja, the question I had cooked up.

"Here, Sir," Tom said handing the question to the Chief Secretary "is a question sent to us by one Member of Parliament which we must find an answer to, before Parliament reconvenes. The Minister has urged me to prepare an answer vehemently denying the allegations implied by the question. But I can assure you, sir, that everything said in this question is correct."

He handed him the note from Msokonde which urged him to deny the allegations in Shedrick's question. Mr. Mkangama read the question and Msokonde's note silently and shook his head again.

"We must stop this man from doing the government further harm. I will advise his Excellency about it," the Chief Secretary said, folding the pieces of paper he had been reading. I'll keep the complementary slips and Mr. Yalomba's question for discussion with the President."

The interview was over, and Tom left the Chief Secretary's Office feeling he had accomplished what needed accomplishing. You may recall that he had once told me that if it came to a showdown between him and his Minister, the latter would have no leg to stand on. Now as he strode along the corridor he knew that he had finished Msokonde once for all.

A week after Tom's interview with the Chief Secretary curious Dar es Salaam residents were startled to read in the *Daily News* and *Uhuru* that there had been a major shake up of the top leadership of the civil service. Only cabinet Ministers had been spared. The sad part of the news item was that the Permanent Secretary of the Ministry of Lands and Environment, Mr. Tom Nyirenda, had been demoted and moved to the Ministry of Energy and Minerals as Commissioner for Minerals, a position he had held years ago.

In his office, Minister Msokonde chuckled to himself when he read the newspaper article. "I was sure the President wouldn't let me down," he said. "But I never expected him to act so fast."

He then lifted his telephone and rang Tom.

"Hallo," he said, "could you come over to my office, please?"

"I'll be with you right away," Tom answered.

In a few minutes Tom was sitting in Msokonde's office. This time he parted with the usual etiquette by smoking in the Minister's Office without asking for permission. He inserted the cigarette in the expensive gilded holder he had bought in Sweden, and lit up using an expensive cigarette lighter.

The Minister said, "I'm sorry about this, Tom."

"About what?"

" This transfer of yours, and especially the demotion you've suffered."

"But that's what you wanted, isn't it? Remember you said in Ambassador Mhina's sitting room that the President would have to decide between removing me or you from this Ministry? He has now ruled in your favour. So why are you sorry?" Tom said, puffing at his golden cigarette holder and causing clouds of smoke to rise in the air. He continued, "Let me assure you, I'm not at all bitter about it. You were quite right in expressing your indignation about the happenings in Sweden, and I suppose you were justified in speaking to the President about me. But what I hate is your hypocrisy. I must tell you quite plainly that you are a stinking hypocrite. You engineer my removal and my demotion, and then you have audacity of telling me that you are sorry about what's happened! This kind of behaviour is worse than that of a person who falls out of a group to visit a trusted friend. Whereas my visit to the friend in Sweden has paid huge dividends, your behaviour may one day lead you into a blind alley."

Msokonde had no idea what Tom meant by saying that his visit to a friend in Sweden had paid huge dividends, and he did not have the guts to ask Tom to explain what he meant by that. The plain truth is that although Msokonde was a politician of sorts, and could articulate his ideas among the unschooled, he always cut a sorry figure when it came to carrying out a sustained argument with people of Tom's intellectual stature. All he could do at this meeting with Tom was to stare at him vacantly.

He did however, mumble something to the effect that although he had told the President about Tom's behaviour while in Sweden he had not suggested a demotion.

Tom released a final spiral of smoke into the air and walked out of the Minister's office.

The following few days were days when government activities virtually came to a halt as Permanent Secretaries, Commissioners and Departmental heads changed places. During such days no major decisions can be made. Officers spend time clearing their desks, handing over duties, and removing their personal papers to their new offices.

* * * * *

Tom had snugly settled down in his former office as Commissioner for Minerals, and within the first week of his return, a number of his former friends including, of course, the local representatives of Wickman's companies of Lukalasi, Mpepo, Matombo and Mahenge had been to his office.

Two weeks had passed since the resuffle of the senior civil servants, and there was another bomb shell - a major cabinet reshuffle. Five new faces of Ministers had been brought into the cabinet. The number of ministers had been reduced from twenty four to eighteen. Among the casualties was the minister for Lands and Environment, Peter Msokonde. Apart from dropping him from the cabinet, not a word had been said about Msokonde, not even the promise of giving him another job, or of returning him to party headquarters from where he had come, since the party was just then carrying out a retrenchment exercise.

It was now Tom's turn to chuckle to himself. Yes, true to his word, Mr. Mkangama had advised the President to act decisively to 'stop Msokonde from doing the government further harm'.

Poor Msokonde, how was he going to cope with life? He had no house, but he had a family of four children and a number of dependents. Indeed, as Tom had predicted, Msokonde had ended up in a blind alley; for had he been a constituent MP he would at least have returned to his constituency and remained in Parliament as a back bencher. But as Msokonde had simply been nominated a national Member of Parliament, no doubt through sycophantic means, his continued presence in Parliament was sure to raise people's eye brows.

12

The reshuffle that had affected many top civil servants and cabinet Ministers and caused untold misery to Peter Msokonde had not affected parastatal organisations, which meant that I was safe at ILD, at least for the time being.

I rang David from my house one afternoon and invited him to my house for a drink and a chat that evening, if he was free. I told him I preferred to see him alone so we could continue the conversation which was cut short just before we boarded the plane at Stockholm airport. David promptly accepted the invitation. I knew he would, not only because drink was involved, but also because of his deference to me.

At seven o'clock that evening, David parked his little Volkswagen outside my house. My houseboy, Moses, had placed a small table and chairs for us outside, at the back of the house, and both David and I relaxed to a very informal chat. My wife, Martha, joked with David about this and that, and retreated into the kitchen to prepare us something to eat while Moses brought us a tray of drinks.

David swept his eyes over the tray and called my wife, "Madam Principal, come quickly there's an accident!" I started laughing, for I understood what he meant. I had seen David making that kind of joke before.

Martha rushed out of the kitchen to where we were sitting, alarm registered over her face, "What's the matter?" she asked. But seeing me laughing she calmed down. "You naughty boys," she said, "I almost spilled the soup I'm preparing. What's the accident?"

"*Konyagi* is nowhere to be seen in the tray, madam, and I call that a major accident," David told Martha, pointing his finger at the tray of drinks.

"He's the culprit," she said pointing at me. There are at least three Konyagi bottles in the house. I asked him if we should bring one, but he said only beer would do. You see, Chris and I are not used to hard drinks. So if we happen to have *Konyagi*, whisky or brandy we keep them for guests only."

"Honoured guests," I corrected.

"How about me, am I not an honoured guest?" David countered.

"By 'honoured guests' we mean those who are from outside ILD," I said. "This is our so called stipulative definition of 'honoured guests', if my knowledge of philosophy still serves me right."

"That may be your stipulative definition, but it is certainly erroneous. You see, to be invited to the Principal's house is to be greatly honoured. I have been invited to the Principal's house. Therefore, I am an honoured guest. This is a simple straightforward syllogism, if you really studied a bit of logic," David said with an air of triumph.

"You win," I said.

"Yes, he wins," Martha agreed; and she told Moses to hurry up and bring a bottle of *Konyagi*.

Moses brought the *Konyagi*, and Martha asked, "How do you want it, David?"

"With tonic, thank you."

This problem sorted out, we settled down to serious talk, he drinking his *Konyagi* gin and tonic, and I, drinking Stella Artois while Martha returned to the kitchen.

"Perhaps you will now tell me more about your wife. Were you serious when you said that lady was your long lost wife?"

"The lady you saw boarding the plane with me is my wife Tsala Chambakare. With all these changes going on I was waiting for you to settle down before I host a small party to introduce her to the ILD community."

"How come she happened to be in Sweden when, as you had told me, she was living with another man in Kondowe?"

"It's a long story, Mr. Principal. When I was incarcerated for a time in prison because of my political activism, Tsala eloped with Mr. Mwampakati who was a member of the Central Committee of the KPP, the Kondowe People's Party which was the ruling party.

"To tell you the truth, Tsala herself was a staunch supporter of the ruling party. She was in fact, chairperson of the women's league at the University of Kondowe. The women's league was an affiliate of the KPP. As a matter of fact, the party derived much of its strength and popularity from the women's league.

"On many occasions I was at loggerheads with Tsala because of our differing political beliefs. I was pro-democracy, she was for the kind of absolutism that characterized the status quo. The President of Kondowe was vested with near dictatorial powers, and Tsala liked that state of affairs, arguing that governance was more efficient under such a system than in a system where vital decisions are often left in the hands of too many people, including ignoramuses.

"What was happening in our country, particularly through the instrumentality of the women's league and the so called young pioneers, was the creation of a personality cult round the President. I was totally opposed to this.

"So, Tsala used to meet party bosses at various meetings, and as you know, it is very easy to cross the boundary that separates decency from familiarity. We'll leave that aside for a moment. The fact is that while Tsala was busy organizing the women's league, I and a few other intellectuals were busy organizing our clandestine movement known as the KLD - Kondowe League for Democracy, which was later to develop as the Kondowe Democratic Party (KDP). When my activities became known to the authorities I was thrown out of the University of Kondowe, and later incarcerated in prison.

"It was at this time that Mwampakati decided to step into my shoes. In a matter of weeks, Tsala moved house and went to live with Mwampakati. Now while Tsala was cohabiting with Mwampakati it transpired that the women's league organised a study tour of Scandinavian countries, to see certain aspects of women's organisations there. Tsala of course, was chosen as the natural leader of the group.

"Unfortunately, or fortunately, depending on whether you are on Mwampakati's or my side, while Tsala and her group were in Sweden Mwampakati fell foul of the President, and he was stripped of all power, and thrown not only out of the Central Committee, but also out of the ruling party itself.

"What had happened is that while Tsala had moved from our house to Mwampakati's, she had inadvertently taken with her lots of my secret papers in which our clandestine party had outlined a step by step Action Plan for the eventual take over of power through democratic means. Our Action Plan stated quite categorically that the use of violent means to overthrow the existing regime was out of the question, because we realized that wherever violent means had been used to overthrow a government, these countries never regained peace. Instead, such countries only experienced coups, reprisals and blood shed. We did not like that to happen in our country.

"Now while Tsala was in Europe, Mwampakati in his carelessness, had left his house under the care of a houseboy who in turn had left the house unlocked. Young pioneers who had been detailed to keep Mwampakati's house under surveillance stormed the house and confiscated some papers, including those containing our Action Plan. It should not surprise you to hear that top party bosses are under surveillance. This is, in fact, the order of the day in Kondowe, where everyone is suspect.

"So poor Mwampakati, my *mtwasi* (*mtwasi* is a male person who marries from the same family as yourself) had lost everything, and much as he tried to defend himself by saying that those papers could have been brought into his house inadvertently by Tsala, no one believed him. In any case, even if that were true, why didn't he destroy them? To say that he didn't know those papers were in his house would be to admit that he was not careful about what was going on in his own house. So either way, he was the loser.

"The most sensible thing Mwampakati did after his mighty fall, was to contact Tsala by all available means and apprise her of these sad developments at home, and advise her not to return home, but if possible, to seek political asylum in any of the Scandinavian countries. In a few month's time, one thing led to another, and Mwampakati was thrown in the same prison where I had been.

"Tsala chose Sweden; and after going through the rigors of acquiring refugee status she was accepted in Sweden. It was then that she started corresponding with me, since she had known all along that I had found a job at ILD in Dar es Salaam. So, Mr. Principal, when you said to me that we would be going to Sweden, I was more than delighted. I wrote to Tsala immediately informing her about our impending visit, and we also talked on the phone several times and worked out all the details of where and when we would meet. That's why you couldn't see me from Saturday to Monday morning before our departure from Sweden. Tsala had actually picked me up from Diplomat Hotel that Saturday morning, and we went to her hostel. As the authorities had already issued her with a ticket, all we did was to ensure that she had a seat on that plane. On arrival at Dar airport there was no problem, as you noticed, since my passport is one of those which include whole families."

David finished his story and took a long draught of his *Konyagi* gin and tonic.

"Is Mwampakati still in prison?" I asked.

"No, he was released after a while, and he ran to South African where he's been organizing some kind of political party in exile."

"How about your clandestine organization, is it likely to come to something or has it disintegrated?"

"Oh, no. It hasn't disintegrated. In fact, it is gaining momentum day by day. We've followers here, in Malawi, Zambia, Zimbabwe, Mozambique, and almost all the capitals of Europe.

"So you hope to be what, some day?"

"To tell you the truth, I have no political ambitions. All I want is to see Kondowe having a democratically installed government. If I'm offered a Ministerial portfolio someday, I'll take it, of course. If I'm not, I'll be content teaching Maths at the University of Kondowe."

"David, let's agree on this question of hosting a party to welcome Mrs. Chambakare. Don't you think I'd better host it rather than yourself? You see, if Martha and I did it, we would tell the others that we were welcoming Tsala to the Institute community. This would make much sense. But if you hosted it what would you say?"

"Yeah, I see your point. It won't be in good taste to invite people to my house and ask them to shake hands with my wife because she is a new comer to the community."

We finally agreed that Martha and I should host the party to welcome Tsala to the ILD Community.

* * * * *

Four months had passed since our return from Sweden. Some of the equipment and teaching materials we had ordered through SIDA began to arrive. One of the staff we recruited at Upsalla University also arrived. The rest were to arrive in three months time.

No bill of lading for the Landrover from Hanson had arrived, and I knew that my letter to Hanson had scared him, and that I had dealt the temptation a deathblow. That gave me peace of mind.

Things were definitely looking up at ILD. The ailing Department of Environmental Studies had been strengthened by newly recruited staff. Essential equipment was in place and David's drinking habit was changing for the better, now that he had discarded the bachelor's garb. My wife Martha was now driving a brand new Volvo, part of the property I had acquired when I rose from a jack to a king.

As time went on, however, it became increasingly difficult for me to continue as Principal of ILD while taking care of my other interests born of my sudden rise into wealth. I had therefore no alternative but to tender my resignation as Principal of ILD.

Part Two

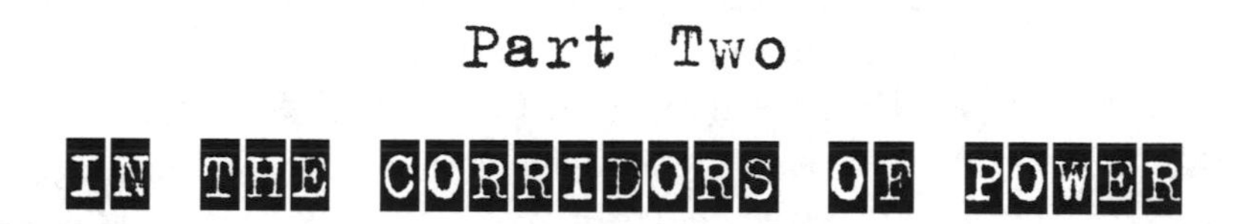

13

The year following my resignation from ILD was an election year not only in Tanzania but also in Kondowe. Three years earlier both Tanzania and Kondowe had formally introduced political pluralism as opposed to the former single party system which had held sway for the past thirty years.

This then was the first time both countries were holding elections under multipartism. It so happened that in Kondowe the ruling Kondowe People's Party, (KPP) had been roundly beaten at the polls, and the Kondowe Democratic Party, (KDP) had emerged as the winner.

For two months preceding the election, David Chambakare had been granted leave of absence from ILD in order to campaign as a parliamentary candidate for his home constituency of Lusuma, on a KDP ticket. As expected, he had trounced the other candidates including the KPP candidate, and had subsequently been offered a cabinet post as Minister for Trade and Industries. David then had duly resigned from his post at ILD and returned to Kondowe.

In Tanzania things were slightly different. Here the ruling party had managed to win with a slender majority, the result of which was to force the party to form a coalition government, since, although it had a slender edge over the opposition parties, it would have been impossible for its government to function effectively without including some members of the opposition parties in the cabinet. It was also widely rumoured that the ruling party had rigged the elections, otherwise, its archrival, the Tanzania National Convention, TNC, would have won.

As a result of the changed circumstances not only was there a sprinkling of members of the opposition parties in the cabinet, but the civil service as a whole, had greatly been affected. Old guards like Permanent Secretaries, Commissioners and Heads of Departments, had given way to new blood; new Ministries had been created, and some old Ministries had been abolished or amalgamated with others.

Old Mr. Oswald Mkangama, the former Chief Secretary, had duly retired, and Tom Nyirenda had been booted out as Commissioner for Minerals, since his Ministry had been amalgamated with that of Lands to form a mammoth Ministry of Lands, Water and Minerals. But one of the luckiest people in the new set up had been Mr. Shedrick Yalomba, the MP for Unyanja. As noted earlier, he had been appointed Deputy Minister for Public Affairs; but after what had been popularly known as 'multiparty elections, he had been named full cabinet Minister of the mammoth, Ministry of Lands, Water and Minerals.

Three years after Tom had left the civil service he launched his hotel business at Mikocheni in Dar es Salaam. True to his dream, he had sold all his property in Stockholm, and had used the proceeds to set up a lucrative hotel business.

Tom had subsequently invited me to team up with him in this business, and I had accepted the invitation. But I did not join Tom as a pauper. Far from it; I also contributed to the business part of the endowment I had acquired in Sweden and we had expanded our business by building a second tourist class hotel on Ngindo Island in Lake Nyasa.

The beautiful island that Msokonde had once intended to sell to Mr. Van-Meer of Johannesburg now belonged to us. Indeed, acquiring the island of Ngindo presented no problem to us as Tom, coming as he did from Mbambay which is close by, was able to trace his ancestry back to the time when his great great grandfather who used to live on the island. So Tom easily acquired that island on the basis of customary land law.

The hotel on Ngindo island which we simply called Ngindo hotel, was intended to be a weekend resort for the growing population of the mining villages of Mpepo on the Matengo highlands, Lukalasi, and the upcoming Mkili and Mbaha villages along the Lake, as well as a tourist resort. For this reason we had bought a small pantoon to ferry patrons from the sandy beach to the island and we had all sorts of swimming paraphernalia: goggles, water skiing gear and aqua-lungs. We had employed people highly qualified in hotel work: hotel management, housekeeping, cooking and so on.

On top of our responsibilities as hoteliers Tom and I were also Board members of Wickman's companies of Mpepo and Lukalasi, in which old Mr. Mkangama also sat. I won't go into details with regard to the remuneration we got from Wickman's companies. Suffice it to say that for the first time in my life I started to experience what it feels like moving in the corridors of power.

It was mid-morning on Saturday and expensive cars started streaming into the parking lot of the Dar es Salaam Sheraton. A Board Meeting of one of Wickman's companies was scheduled to take place in the Kongoni room of the Sheraton that morning. The Kongoni room was one of the three most exclusive and most elegant conference rooms in the Sheraton. Situated on the twelfth floor of the hotel, Kongoni room gave a breathtaking view of the Indian Ocean with its chain of coral islands in the distance.

Linda Wickman and a goliath of a man stood at the entrance to Kongoni room to usher in the incoming Board Members. Linda had flown from Sweden specifically to chair this meeting in place of her father who had flown to South America to chair another meeting. The thickset man standing beside Linda was her bodyguard, so Linda told me afterwards. It appears that since Linda's abduction, it had been agreed within the Wickman family that each of the three family members should have an armed body guard whenever they were in a situation when abduction was remotely possible. Come to think about it, this kind of existence must be hell, since privacy is no longer possible.

When Tom and I approached the entrace to Kongoni hall Linda had to restrain herself from giving each of us a bear hug. Had she done so, not only would the other Board members, including old Mkangama, have felt ill at ease, but the goliath would have been embarrassed, and who knows what he might have done? As it was, Linda simply gave her characteristic captivating smile and showed us in.

There were only two items on the agenda for the meeting: to discuss the Company's audited accounts for the past fiscal year, and to receive a technical report from a team of experts who had done mineral prospecting along the Lake Nyasa littoral.

The Balance sheet showed huge dividends which had accrued to the Government as one of the shareholders in the Company and the other shareholders, including Mr. Wickman himself who was the majority shareholder, had also realized huge profits.

"Madam chair," observed Mr.Mkangama who, as a retired former Chief Secretary, had been appointed on contract to represent the Government on the Board of Directors of Wickman's company. "If all the foreign companies were operating as profitably as this Company, and giving Caesar his due as this Company is doing, Tanzania would not be numbered among the LDCs."

"Thank you for the complement Mr.Mkangama," Linda Wickman said. "I really don't see why Tanzania should be numbered among the LDCs. This country's potential is so great that I wouldn't be surprised if in a few years' time Tanzania became a great industrialized nation."

"I agree with you Madam chair, that the potential is great," I said. " But the fact remains that we are among the LDC's. What I think we must do is diversify the economy. To think that the World Bank should regard Tanzania as being among the poorest nations in the world is scandalous!"

"Have they really said so?" Linda asked.

"It was in the papers yesterday," I answered.

Tom continued, "I agree with you Chris. I think in the past there's been undue emphasis on agriculture. It's true, agriculture is important and we need to continue developing some areas, especially in Southern Tanzania by introducing mechanized farming, and doing away with the traditional hand hoe. I am sure if that could be done, Southern Tanzania could be turned into an important maize belt. But that does not mean we should neglect other economic ventures like industries, mining and so on."

An economist who had accompanied Linda from Sweden concurred with Nyirenda. He said, "It is a known fact among economists that no country can expect to reach a high level of development by relying exclusively on agriculture. Of course, agriculture is essential, but for a real break through in development a sizable percentage of the population must be released to engage in other economic activities like mining, light and heavy industries, tourism, commerce, and so on."

The whole morning session was used for discussing the audited accounts of the company. During the lunch break all the Board members moved to an executive room where lunch was served. As the meeting was to continue in the afternoon, the business lunch was a light one consisting only of soup, followed by the main course. Those who wanted could also have a glass of table wine or beer. This was to ensure that the afternoon session would not be hampered by some members dozing off as a result of having taken too heavy a meal.

The afternoon session started promptly at 3 p.m. The Board was to discuss and receive a technical report prepared by a team of experts who had been commissioned to carry out mineral prospecting in some areas along Lake Nyasa littoral. The team consisted of Mr. Jacob Palme, a Swede, Mr. Abdulnur of Asian extraction and Mr. Steve Lweno, a Tanzanian.

The experts were on top of their job. Using an overhead projector they showed the geological structure of the area they had surveyed using the most up-to-date methods of remote sensing. They explained that the same rock formation seen in the Luilo area near Manda, extended southward to the Mbaha/Mkili areas. Infact, they said, the kimberlite pipe seen at Luilo which yielded industrial diamonds when mined in the late 1960's extended as far south as Mkili along Lake Nyasa and somewhere near the villages of Mkili and Mbaha at the base of the Livingstone range of mountains, they had discovered not only industrial diamonds but also rubies, and other precious gemstones.

As a result of this excellent exposition by the experts, a sub-committee of the Board was set up consisting of Linda Wickman, Tom Nyirenda, Mr. Mkangama, the Swedish Economist and myself. This sub-committee was to see Mr. Shedrick Yalomba, the Minister for Lands, Water and Minerals, and hold high level talks with him and his team, about starting mining operations in the newly discovered areas.

The afternoon session ended at 5 p.m. but a few minutes before the Chairperson declared the meeting closed, a young secretary walked into the hall carrying a brief case. The chairperson interrupted her summing up of the proceedings by saying, "Gentlemen, this is as good a point as I could have wished to reach at which to declare the meeting closed, for I can see Yvonne ready to crown our deliberations with our sitting allowance."

With that remark by the chairperson, the young secretary opened the brief case and fished out a piece of paper on which our names had been neatly typed, and against each name was the figure 200 USD, which was equivalent to Tshs. 200,000. All we were required to do was put our signatures against our names and Yvonne passed on to each one of us an envelope containing 200 USD.

I could see old Mkangama chuckling inwardly as he pocketed his envelope. Two hundred US dollars by our standards, was a lot of money for having attended a meeting which had lasted barely four hours! This was indeed a far cry from the days I used to spend whole days at ILD Board meetings, only to end up with Tshs. 2,000 per meeting, even if the meeting lasted for more than one day. Mkangama, Tom and I reached the undeclared consensus that we were now moving in the corridors of power!

Before we actually filed out of the conference hall, Linda announced that there was going to be a dinner at 7.30 p.m.

At around 7.15 p.m. members of the Board of Wickman's Company, some of whom accompanied by their wives, began to arrive at the Sheraton, ready for the sumptuous dinner earlier announced by Linda Wickman. Among the dignitaries, this time, were also a few government Ministers and their wives, including of course, Mr. Shedrick Yalomba and his wife. There were also one or two Permanent Secretaries including Mr. Yalomba's Permanent Secretary, the newly appointed Commissioner for Minerals, and the three experts who had made the technical presentation to the Board in the afternoon.

This time, the dinner was being served in another exclusive hall of the hotel - the Summit. Normally this hall of the Sheraton was used for State banquets during the visits of foreign heads of State. But occasionally the hotel management allowed it to be used by high powered business executives such as Board members of Wickman's Company, which could afford to pay in advance the 2,000 USD for hire of the Summit.

I would be deluding myself if I imagined that as a result of my description of it, the uninitiated could conceive a realistic picture of the Summit. It is only those who actually move in the corridors of power, those who, so to speak, rub shoulders with the privileged in society, that can grasp the picture I am trying to convey. Suffice it to say that the elegance of the Summit belies any attempt on my part to describe it adequately. The expensive chandeliers hanging like stalactites from a ceiling made of some modern building material I knew not what; the walls made of the same exotic material as that used for the ceiling; the expensive wall to wall carpet and furniture, not to mention the glittering silver, China and glass ware; the immaculately clean table cloths and serviettes, made me feel humble and undeserving.

When I introduced my wife Martha to Linda at the door, Linda embraced her, and wiped a tear. She whispered to her, "I owe your husband a big debt."

"I Know," Martha said, "I'm proud he did it."

As we walked towards the seats we were shown, Martha whispered to me, "Now I understand why you fret about cleanliness at home. You people often see places like this, and you think you can transfer them to your own homes!"

"In a way you're right, darling," I said. "After you've been to a place like this, and you return home only to be greeted by flies, dust and litter, you really become mad."

"Sh, sh, sh!!" Martha hissed with a finger across her lips. "Surely you do not mean we're all that dirty, do you?"

"Of course, not. But sometimes when Moses forgets to dust the furniture in the house, or to arrange things properly, I feel most uncomfortable. I always think of places like this one, and many others I've been to."

Martha held my hand and whispered again, "I don't know some of these people. Can you tell me who they are?"

"O.K." I whispered to her. "You know Mr. Yalomba, alright. The gentleman with a small beard is Mr. Oswald Mkangama.... The tall slender gentleman at the corner is the Permanent Secretary in Mr. Yalomba's Ministry...."

And so I went through all the names of the dignitaries my wife wanted to know: the Ministers, the Permanent Secretaries, the Commissioners, the business tycoons, and some of the Board members.

We settled in our seats. Minister Yalomba sat on the right handside of Linda Wickman; that is to say, at the head of the table. The other Ministers also sat close to Linda. Martha and Mrs. Yalomba made sure they sat next to each other, since they wanted to gossip in Kimpoto, their vernacular, while enjoying their dinner. As a matter of fact, both Martha and Mrs. Yalomba came from the same village on the shores of Lake Nyasa. But on this occasion what made it imperative that they should sit together was that whereas Martha was a high school graduate, Mrs. Yalomba had not even completed primary education, and so she could not understand a sentence of English, let alone speak one. So Martha wanted to avert any embarrassment should one occur, if any of the white men at table addressed Minister Yalomba's wife in English! Martha would come in handy as an interpreter.

I was sandwiched between old Mrs. Mkangama and Mrs. Nyirenda. Whereas I found it comfortable talking with Susan Nyirenda who, as already recorded, was a family friend, it was rather difficult to break the ice between Mrs. Mkangama and myself. Not only was she an elderly lady, but as the wife of a former Chief Secretary I did not quite know what the demands of etiquette required me to do under the circumstances. How should I address her? Could I make jokes with her? Fortunately for me, Mr. Mkangama was sitting directly opposite his wife, and most of the time the couple were talking to one another.

From my vantage point I could see Minister Shedrick Yalomba gesticulating as he was conversing with Linda Wickman in rather halting English. I could also hear Mrs. Yalomba asking Martha in Kimpoto, the local vernacular spoken along some parts of Lake Nyasa littoral, which spoon, or which knife she should use! Both Susan and I laughed quietly when we heard this.

"The small one near you on your left hand side," Martha would answer in Kimpoto. Later we heard Martha say in Kimpoto, "Use the toothed knife on your right handside."

The truth is simply that the display of silver and glassware on the tables was bewildering, and the meal, what a meal it was! I bet neither Martha nor Susan, nor Mrs. Yalomba had ever been to a dinner as rich as this one. I couldn't say the same about Mrs. Mkangama, for it is possible or most likely that when Mr. Mkangama was Chief Secretary she may have been to State banquets, or she may have accompanied her husband on overseas trips. But as for the three ladies from Unyanja whom I've mentioned, I was sure this kind of dinner was their first experience, even though Susan had been wife of a Permanent Secretary, and Mrs. Yalomba wife of a Minister! The point is that Mr. Yalomba had been a Deputy Minister for the last two years, and only after the recent elections had he been appointed a full Cabinet Minister, and wives of Deputy Ministers are not normally invited to State banquets, nor are the wives of Permanent Secretaries.

On a platform at one end of the hall a small band was playing sweet soothing music. But what really entertained the diners was the soft captivating voice of a young lady called Miriam whenever she took the microphone to sing some favourite songs.

The dinner consisted of an appetizer in the form of prawns in thick sauce. These were served in beautiful glasses, which looked like small chalices. In fact it was these small glasses which prompted Mrs. Yalomba to ask Martha, in Kimpoto, of course, whether the prawns were to be drunk or to be eaten with a spoon, and Martha had replied that the small spoon on the left hand side was meant for that purpose! Then there was soup; to be exact, there was a choice of soups: mashroom, Tomato, consommé, minestrone etc. The soup was to be taken with rolls of bread and butter made in South Africa, of all countries. The main course followed. The two-page menu had all kinds of dishes: African, English, German, Italian, French, Swedish, Chinese and Indian. There were sea foods of every kind: lobster themidor, kingfish, whole changu, flat fish, fish muniere etc. There were meats of every kind: fillet steak, lamb and pork chops, sirloin steak, fried chicken, turkey, oxtail, tongue and so on. Indeed the menu was so bewildering that I could hear Mrs. Yalomba telling Martha, "You choose anything for me. Whatever you will have, I will have the same."

As the dinner progressed one could sense the atmosphere of enjoyment as people's conversation became more and more animated as a result of the white and red table wine people were consuming.

Dessert followed towards the end of the dinner. Again there was a wide choice: cream of caramel, fruit salad, rich cake served with cream, and so on. As if this was not enough, some people ended up eating cheese and biscuits and capping the whole meal with different types of liquor or coffee.

It was around 11.30 p.m. that we staggered to our cars after what had definitely been an enjoyable evening. As we were driving home from the dinner, Martha said to me, "Darling, I was seeing many of those people for the first time today: the Ministers and Permanent Secretaries about whom we read in the papers so often."

"That's what happens when you begin moving in the corridors of power," I said, concentrating on the wheel.

"How do you mean, the corridors of power?"

"Well, when we were at ILD, were you ever invited to a dinner like the one you have just had? When your friend Grace, Shedrick's wife, was drying small fish or dagaa back home in Liuli before Shedrick climbed up the political ladder, did she ever experience such things as to night's dinner? That's what I mean by moving in the corridors of power. You get to a situation, which allows you to rub shoulders with dignitaries. You move among people who make vital decisions which affect whole nations."

"Yes, I now see what you mean. I have often wondered, for instance, why it is that whenever there are State banquets, it's the same people who are invited. The rest of us only follow the proceedings of the banquets on the radio!"

"There you are! Those are the people who move in the corridors of power. Normally the same people keep meeting at all important gatherings. Let me give you an example: there are individuals in our country who sit in the Central Committee of the ruling Party; in the National Executive Committee; in the Parliament, and in the Cabinet. Such people will find themselves automatically invited to every important gathering being held in the country."

"I suppose," Martha said, "these people become friends, willy nilly, being forced as they are, to find themselves together so often."

"Not necessarily. What they often do is establish some kind of 'modus vivendi' in order to retain their status quo."

"What' re you talking about, Chris? Is that Latin?"

"Sorry, those are Latin phrases which have been anglicized, if you like. Establishing a modus vivendi simply means tolerating a mode of living as a temporary expedient in order to get by in life, or as I have said, in order to retain the status quo, the existing position. The truth is that sometimes they hate one another, they backbite one another, they despise one another and so on. But in public, they put on masks of civility and gentility."

Martha retorted, "But I have on some occasions watched some of these big people outside Parliament building: the way they greet one another; the way they pat one another on the shoulders; the way they talk. I've always been impressed. I think our leaders show marks of friendship, at least among themselves."

"I am telling you, Darling, that that's part of the game. They all want to retain their positions. You can't retain your position when you don't know who is on the line; when you show clearly that you are the odd man out. You have got to behave like everybody else, otherwise nobody will select you for this or that important committee."

"So that's what you call moving in the corridors of power?"

"Yeah, you must know whom to see and talk to; you must know what phrase to use and when, and so on."

"But Chris, if as you said before, it's the same people who keep meeting in different forums, isn't it a good thing that this enables them to speak with one voice, that this makes for solidarity among them?"

"Martha, you are raising an extremely controversial point. You should have gone to university to do Political Science."

"Don't make me angry now, Chris! Wasn't it you who cut short my studies? You were in a hurry to marry me!"

"Sorry about that, baby. But let me come back to your question. It is true that a government must have internal cohesion, solidarity or unity, if you like. An issue is brought to the Cabinet. Members of the Cabinet are free to discuss it, put forward differing arguments, analyze it, tear it apart, reject it or accept it. But once a matter of public policy is agreed upon by the majority, then the whole Cabinet must accept it. This is what is known as collective responsibility, which governs the conduct of government, at least according to the Westminster model of democracy. But the danger I see in our system here, of the same people sitting in all the Party and State organs, is the encouragement of inbreeding of ideas. Meaningful cross-fertilization of ideas hardly ever takes place in our system, because there are no new ideas. The same people, with the same limited knowledge - these people cannot be expected to propel the nation into the next century.

"What I really feel, myself, is that there is need to expand democracy as much as possible by including in the various government organs, people with as many shades of opinions as possible. Especially now that there is political pluralism, the ruling Party should not hesitate to put in government talented people whatever their political leanings."

I finished my little lecture to Martha as we were entering the gate to our house at Kimara. I parked the Volvo in the garage, and rejoined Martha on the steps of the house. Moses who had just locked the gate of the fence came to where we were standing and asked Martha if he should serve us food. It was nearly midnight then. Martha looked at Moses and said, "You must be joking, Moses. How can you talk about giving us food when we can hardly walk because of the heavy stomachs? And look, this is a quarter to twelve mid-night. Who can eat at such a late hour?"

So saying, Martha who had a bunch of the keys to the house in her handbag, opened the door leading into the sitting room, and put on the light. As I was crossing the sitting room to the bedroom, I noticed that the sitting room was not in top form: the pillows on the seats, the paintings on the walls were not properly arranged. I just looked at these things without saying a word.

Martha had read my mind. It is said that when you have lived with a wife for a longtime a kind of clairvoyance or mind reading develops between you. Your wife knows what you are thinking about and you know what she has in mind even before a word is uttered.

Martha said, "I know you are comparing our home with the Sheraton Summit".

"Of course, I am," I said. "Look at those paintings hanging awkwardly on the wall. Look at those pillows; look at the carpet!"

Martha simply grinned at me, and disappeared into the bedroom.

14

Hon. Shedrick Yalomba, Minister for Lands, Water and Minerals was sitting at the head of a well-polished *Mninga* table. With him was his newly appointed Permanent Secretary, a young man in his mid thirties; the Commissioner for Minerals who in the past, had been Tom's assistant; another young man who was the Ministry's economist; and a fifth person who, we were told, was the Ministry's legal officer.

Our sub-committee, as noted earlier, consisted of Linda, Tom, Oswald Mkangama and myself. We had also asked Mr. Jacob Palme, one of the experts, to accompany us to this meeting just in case the need arose for someone to give a technical explanation of any point.

Wickman's company had done the prospecting alright, and they had discovered the diamonds and rubies, and they had paid to the government all the prospecting fees as required by law. But all this did not entitle them to start mining right away. The government had the right to enter into some kind of partnership with them, in the so called joint venture arrangement.

To start opening two mines, one for diamonds and the other for rubies, required a substantial capital outlay, not only for plant and machinery, but also for providing the necessary infrastructure like roads, water, electricity and other public utilities.

The discussion at this meeting, therefore centered mainly round what contribution the Tanzania government would make to the joint venture, which in turn would determine who would be the majority shareholder.

Hon. Shedrick Yalomba, of course, had no inkling what these high level economic matters meant. What he kept repeating were the common place platitudes that Tanzania was primarily for Tanzanians and therefore any wealth discovered in Tanzania should primarily benefit indigenous Tanzanians. It was good, he said, for people of other nationalities to assist Tanzania with their technology to exploit her natural resources to the maximum. He also insisted that since the minerals had been discovered in his parliamentary constituency, whatever final arrangements were reached his constituents had to benefit from the mining operations. His constituents had to be employed to provide the unskilled labour, and where possible, the skilled labour as well. He recalled with pride that many of his constituents had worked in gold and diamond mines in South Africa in the 1940s, so he didn't see why they should not be employed to work in the mines at home.

Linda looked at Jacob Palme and at Tom. Then she said, "Of course, Mr. Minister, I sympathize with your sentiments. This country has been blessed with rich resources, and it is only right that its indigenous people should benefit from these resources. But to actually be able to extract these resources, there are certain stubborn facts you must contend with. You must have the know-how; you must have the necessary infrastructures, machinery and, as you rightly suggest, the labour force too; skilled, semi-skilled, and unskilled. I think it is these stubborn facts that we need to address at this meeting. Perhaps, Hon. Minister, you will allow me at this juncture to ask my colleague, Mr. Palme, to go into the technical details so we can all appreciate what we are up against."

The rugged looking Jacob Palme cleared his throat, stood up and unfolded a map he had with him. He started by showing on the map the area being discussed. It was clear from the map that, apart from the narrow dirt road hugging the Lake shore, there was nothing resembling a road anywhere near the area, and the exact location of the minerals, according to Mr. Palme, was several kilometres in the bush away from the dirt road. Thus to dream of starting two mines in the middle of the jungle without first constructing passable roads, was next to madness.

From Palme's map it was clear that the nearest electricity power line of the National Grid was at Makambako, roughly two hundred kilometres away. "Before you could start your two mines, if you were seriously thinking of large scale mining as opposed to small scale scratching of the ground as is normally done by small diggers, you had either to have the National Grid extended to the new area in order to supply you with the necessary electricity, or to build your own thermal power station, or harness hydroelectric power from river Ruhuhu - twenty kilometers away. Whichever way you choose you would require a considerable capital outlay for the project." The map showed that the nearest water mains was at Mbinga, forty kilometers away. For any meaningful development to take place in these *Miyombo* covered foothills, it was necessary to have water piped either from river Ruhuhu, or pumped from the lake, either way, the cost involved would be considerable.

Palme went on to describe the kinds of equipment needed to start a mine: the heavy drilling machines, the stone crushers and so on.

"Mr. Minister," said Mr. Mkangama as soon as Palme had finished speaking, "technology is technology, and economics will always remain economics. I suppose these are the stubborn facts the lady was referring to earlier. You can talk about your constituents having priority of consideration when it comes to employing people in the mines; and you can talk about Tanzania's natural resources being used primarily by Tanzanians, but kimberlite pipes and quartzite will remain hard; and to crush them up you need heavy crushers, not hammers and hoes! What contribution can our government make to the enterprise?"

"Yes," agreed the young economist who was there to advise the Minister. "I think this is a matter we must address. Perhaps our expert Mr. Palme can tell us what he thinks the total capital outlay is likely going to be."

"But you are an economist, aren't you?" Retorted Mr. Mkangama. "You are the one who should tell us what the outlay is likely going to be, and in fact, in the end you will have to tell us what contribution your Ministry can make to the whole undertaking. That's what is going to determine whether the government will be the majority shareholder or not."

The young economist answered, "I am sorry, Sir, I can't say anything about these things since I'm an Agricultural economist, not an Industrial economist."

"Then what are you doing in this Ministry?" Thundered Mr. Mkangama. Everybody round the table except perhaps Mr. Palme, who knew that Mkangama had, for many years, been the Chief Secretary and head of the Civil Service. Therefore, even though he was now retired, his words at this meeting carried that extra weight characteristic of the words of people in authority. Psychologists would say the words still had a halo effect.

Mr. Mkangama continued, "Hon. Minister, when I was Chief Secretary I exercised special care to minimize misallocation of manpower, especially of highly trained manpower, in our Ministries. But here you have a chap trained as an agricultural economist purpoting to assist you with problems, which are essentially industrial! I will talk to Bill Duwe about this, for we seem to be slipping back to the old mistake of haphazardly placing people in Ministries."

Now, Bill Duwe was Mr. Mkangama's successor as Chief Secretary. Minister Yalomba and his subordinates knew that Mkangama was still in a position to influence top level decisions in government, since he was often invited to advise the President on crucial matters of State. In particular,

Mkangama had great influence on the new Chief Secretary who regarded Mkangama as his godfather, knowing that he had risen to this position of eminence because of Mkangama's strong recommendation to the President.

So when Mr. Mkangama questioned the young economist's presence in the Ministry of Lands, Water and Minerals his remarks sent a wave of fear in the young economist's spine, and he was visibly disturbed.

Unknown to Minister Yalomba and his subordinates, as virtually all of them were new to the Ministry, experts of Wickman's Company had already carried out a comprehensive feasibility study, and they had prepared a detailed Staff Appraisal Report. Linda Wickman now produced two copies of this report and handed them to Mr. Yalomba. Among other things, the report listed the equipment required to start the two mines, and gave the approximate cost of the plant and equipment. It gave details of the infrastructure required and the budget for it; it gave details of the manpower requirements, and it even gave projections of production for the next ten years.

The voluminous report had appendices showing charts of various kinds, technical drawings, price indices and so on. These things of course did not make sense to Hon. Shedrick Yalomba. All he could do was to pass the report to his Permanent Secretary.

The Permanent Secretary said, "Since we are seeing this document for the first time now, we need to study it and make our comments on it. I suggest we give ourselves a month to study the document, and our Ministry will take the initiative to call another meeting to finalize the matter."

"We need two months," said Minister Yalomba. "You see, after we have studied the report in the Ministry we will have to prepare a Cabinet Paper which as you know, will first have to go to the Inter - Ministerial Technical Committee (IMTC) before it goes to the Cabinet. It is the Cabinet which will decide what role the Government will play in this venture. I guess the whole process will take about eight weeks. Let's then fix our next meeting with you nine weeks from today."

"Fair enough," said Linda Wickman. "We will be waiting to hear from you about the next meeting. I do hope, Mr. Minister, that you will treat the matter as expeditiously as possible."

* * * * *

On a Monday morning exactly six weeks after our meeting with officials of the Ministry of Lands, Water and Minerals, Tom rang me to say that Mr. Mkangama had rung him saying that the two of us, Tom and I, Mr. Mkangama himself and Minister Yalomba were required at State House by 9 a.m. the following day. We were to meet His Excellency the President who wanted to discuss with us the question of starting new mining operations at Mkili and Mbaha.

I had never been to the State House before. This was going to be my first official meeting with the President. Indeed it now became clear to me that Tom and I *were* moving in the corridors of power. To have access to Government Ministers like the ones we had at dinner a few months ago, and now the President himself, was to move in the highest echelons of government where vital decisions are made.

We were in our seats at 9 a.m sharp. I learnt for the first time that when you are invited to the State House you do not meet the President in his office. Rather, he meets you in the visitor's hall, which is some distance from his office. Protocol demands that you get seated in your seats some minutes before the host arrives. When he enters the room, you stand up and greet him. Then you sit down after, not before he has sat down.

Mr. Mkangama and Tom, and probably Mr. Yalomba too, knew all these niceties of protocol. So all I had to do was follow what they were doing, and all went well.

It appears that the question of opening the two mines at the base of the Livingstone mountains had been brought to the Cabinet, but it had not yet been decided what contribution the government should make to the venture. In other words, the matter hadn't yet received the President's assent, because the President wasn't sure if the government should be the majority shareholder in the venture or not. The figures were there to look at, and to be sure, they were staggering. Could the government afford to invest so much money on one economic venture when there were so many other demands on the government coffers?

The President had heard the views of his Ministers in the Cabinet, but he still wanted the advice of 'outsiders', as it were. For this reason he asked Mr. Yalomba to hold his peace, and instead he paid attention to what Mkangama and Tom had to say. He also listened to me when I chipped in occasionally, The President knew that the three of us were members of the Board of

Directors of Wickman's Company and he assumed rightly I think, that we had intimate knowledge of the financial standing of the Company. Among other things, the President also wanted to know if Wickman's Company was the kind of company to be trusted to do honest business with the Government.

It took Mr. Mkangama only ten minutes to convince the President about the impeccability of the business record of Wickman's company. He cited the figures released by the recent audited accounts and underscored the fact that unlike any other company he knew, this company had not only made huge profits but it had also paid Caesar all his due. Although he did not mention this, I am sure Mr. Mkangama also thought of the generous sitting allowance given by this Company at its Board Meetings!

The President was convinced. In the end it was agreed that the Tanzania government should be the majority shareholder with 51 per cent of the shares, while Wickman's company would have 49 per cent of the shares.

* * * * *

The meeting promised by Minister Yalomba did take place after ten weeks and it was then disclosed that the Tanzania Government would contribute 51 per cent of the required capital to start the two mines.

While negotiations to start the two mines were still going on between the Tanzania government and Wickman's Company and both the government and Wickman were readying themselves to look for the finances necessary to start operations, our hotel business at Mikocheni in Dar and on Ngindo island in Lake Nyasa was booming.

As Tom's business partner I was shuttling between Dar and Ngindo Island near Mbambabay. Our two mini buses were fully engaged in ferrying patrons between Dar and Ngindo and vice versa. There were also private tour operators who helped boost up our business by transporting tourists to Ngindo.

It was Saturday evening, and I was relaxing in the lounge cum bar of Ngindo Hotel. The lounge was full of people, most of whom having just arrived from the mining villages of Mpepo and Lukalasi, and a few from the new mining sites at Mkili and Mbaha. There were also some who had travelled from Dar.

In a corner of the lounge I spotted an African gentleman seated at a table and talking to a white patron. I thought I knew the African gentleman, but from that distance, I wasn't quite sure of his identity. But as I was part owner of the hotel there was nothing to prevent me from moving round the lounge asking the guests how they were getting on. So I stood up and approached the two gentlemen at the corner. To my delight, or should I say, my astonishment, whom did I see but Mr. Msokonde, the former Minister for Lands and my former student?

"Hi, Peter, how nice to see you!" I said, shaking hands with him.

"Hi, *Mzee*, what a small world," he said, "We haven't met for ages." Then showing me the gentleman he was sitting with he said, "This is Mr. Van-Meer from Johannesburg. He is a longtime friend of mine who was on a visit to Dar es Salaam, and I thought it worth bringing him here so he could see some of our beautiful beaches of Lake Nyasa." Turning to Mr. Van Meer, Peter Msokonde continued, "Mr Van Meer, this is Chris Mayesa who was for a long time Principal of a training institution under my Ministry when I was Minister for Lands. Before then he was my professor at the University of Dar es Salaam."

I shook hands with Mr. Van Meer, and he said, "I am very pleased to visit your beautiful country. As a matter of fact, I have been coming to Tanzania at least once each year during the past five years. I have been to virtually all the national parks in this country, and I have been to these parts of Lake Nyasa twice before."

"You're welcome, Mr. Van Meer," I said. "Do please feel quite at home here."

Now when Peter Msokonde introduced me to his friend he didn't mention the fact that I was the joint owner of the hotel because he had no idea that I was. Like many other people, he thought that this hotel was owned by Tom Nyirenda alone. He also didn't know that I knew about his relationship with Van Meer. Tom Nyirenda, as you will remember, had shown me the note which later landed in the hands of the then Chief Secretary, Mr. Oswald Mkangama, in which Msokonde had sought advice from Tom on the technicalities of selling Ngindo island to a certain Van-Meer of Johannesburg.

So the moment Msokonde mentioned the name of Van Meer, it all came back! A thought crossed my mind that I had to watch out for this man, Van

Meer. Why should Msokonde bring this man to Ngindo Island, the island he had not only coveted, but also actually planned to buy? Could there be any sinister motive still lingering in his mind?

On Sunday morning I went to church in the nearby village of Mapendo on the mainland. I returned to the hotel at about 10 am only to find the hotel almost deserted, except for Msokonde and his guest from Johannesburg. Most of the guests were out either angling, swimming or water skiing.

Van Meer, accompanied by his host, Peter Msokonde, was busy taking photographs of the hotel. They did not see me climb up the steps to the hotel, but I saw them moving from corner to corner of the main hotel building, taking photographs from various angles.

When I appeared around the corner and said, "Hallo!" Van Meer quickly put his camera in its case and showed the signs of irritation of a person caught red-handed.

"How do you like our hotel building?" I asked.

"Oh, very much. Fine Architecture, this; who designed it? I like particularly the African art work used for the doors and the supporting pillars. The large mural in the dining hall is also excellent, and so are the huge Makonde carvings in the garden. I have been taking photographs of these things, so I could try to imitate them back home. You see, I am in hotel business at home, and I think developing something like this would be interesting."

"*Mzee*, did I hear you say our hotel?" Msokonde asked in disbelief. "Do you have a part in this?"

"You didn't know?" I asked teasingly. "I teamed up with your former Permanent Secretary, Tom Nyirenda, to build this hotel."

"I knew that it belongs to Tom because someone told me that it was an off shoot of the Mikocheni Hotel in Dar," Msokonde said. "But I had no idea that you were also involved."

I could see from Msokonde's face that he was internally cursing his rotten chance. Here is a beautiful island which, if things had worked out well, he would have sold to a wealthy South African hotelier, and who knows if that business transaction wouldn't have changed Msokonde's own life? As it was, not only had the plan failed miserably, but the dirty game of politics had landed him where he was now, as a small time tour operator.

Although it may not be in good taste to divulge people's secrets, especially of people who have once held positions of authority such as Ministerial positions, facts always remain stubbornly what they are. It is a fact that Peter Msokonde having suffered his political eclipse was wise enough to revive his old Landrover, and was now engaged in transporting tourists to various destinations. Although he delighted in regarding himself as a tour operator, a title which carried a little more esteem, he was really no more than an ordinary taxi *bubu* driver, if you don't mind calling a Landrover a taxi.

Having seen Van Meer stow away his camera the way he did, I was in no doubt that this man was up to some mischief. Exactly what, I could not tell. Maybe he wanted to copy the plan and layout of our hotel as he had said. But why suddenly stop taking pictures after seeing me, and especially after learning that I was part owner of the hotel?

I made a mental note of all this and alerted the hotel security guards to be extra vigilant that night. I told the chief security guard to specifically keep an eye on the rooms occupied by Van Meer and Peter Msokonde.

Nothing extraordinary happened that Sunday night. After breakfast the following Monday, most of the remaining guests, including Van Meer and Msokonde, left. The Majority of the guests, those from the mining villages in Mbinga district, had left on Sunday afternoon so as to be at their respective work places.

I waved Msokonde and his South African friend goodbye as they entered the pantoon to take them to the shore, and hurriedly retreated into the hotel. The first thing I did was to call three security guards to the rooms vacated by Van Meer and Msokonde. Together we made a thorough inch by inch inspection of the rooms. I had an intuition that these two people might have done something sinister. In fact I feared that Van Meer might have hidden a time bomb somewhere, intending to blow the hotel to pieces. You can never take chances with some people, you know?

We combed the two rooms, the corridors, the nooks and corners, and the surroundings of the hotel, but nothing suspicious was found. Somehow I felt ashamed of myself for having suspected innocent visitors.

15

Four weeks after Van Meers' visit, I was again in the hotel on Ngindo Island. Business was booming as usual, and there were hordes of tourists and mineworkers enjoying themselves in various ways. They came and went according to their plans.

On Sunday, as usual, I went to the little church at Mapendo village. Just as the service was coming to an end, the air was rent by the sound of a big explosion coming from the direction of Ngindo Island nearby. There was pandemonium as the small village congregation scrambled to the door of the little church. Then somebody shouted, "Fire! There's fire on the island! The hotel's on fire!"

All eyes turned towards the lake, and sure enough, thick smoke was belching from a corner of the main hotel building. I felt my knees begin to give way, and my mouth to get dry. Without wasting time I ran to the small Suzuki which I normally used when visiting the island hotel and drove the three old kilometres to where the pantoon had been moored to a post. I steered the Suzuki into the pantoon, and in a few minutes, I was back on the island.

All the hotel workers, including the security guards, cooks and gardeners, were busy fighting the fire. Fortunately we had fire extinguishers at all strategic places in the hotel, and our employees had been drilled on how to fight fires should they break out. So as soon as the fire had started, as a result of short circuit caused by touching wires from the huge power generator we had installed in the hotel, our employees had effectively used the fire extinguishers and braved the fierce fire. Nobody had been injured in the explosion or burnt by the fire that had followed.

By the time I arrived at the scene, the fire had, in fact, effectively been controlled and our people were now dealing with the dying embers of what had been the wooden supporting pillars.

But the explosion had ripped off a large part of the northern wing of the hotel, which consisted of offices, storerooms, and one executive suite which Tom, or I used whenever we stayed at the hotel. This is to say that the room in which I had spent the previous night, the room I had left only a couple of hours earlier when I went to church, had been blown off! Had the explosion occurred, say at 5 or 6 am that morning I would surely have been blown into eternity.

This thought was chilling. Where would I be at this moment had I been blown into bits and pieces? As a firm believer in what Christianity teaches concerning' the last things', namely, judgement and the subsequent eternal life of bliss or banishment, I knew that my undying personality would now be experiencing one of these alternatives. But I had been spared! Indeed, I had been spared miraculously. I was filled with emotion when I remembered the words of Psalm 121, the same words I had once recited in Abisko National Park in Sweden, "*The Lord shall preserve thy going out and thy coming in, from this time forth, and even for evermore.*"

I must confess that ever since I started moving among the higher circles of society, meeting dignitaries of every kind in our two hotels; engaging in negotiations with government officials as a member of the board of directors of Wickman's Company; in a word, moving in the corridors of power, my recitation of Psalm 121 was not as frequent as it used to be in the past. The truth dawned on me that we humans are very fickle and changeable in our resolve to maintain the intimacy with the Lord to which we are called. Get a little more fame; get a little more money than you used to have; get a little more power, and these things quickly get into your head, and behaviour begins to change. Imperceptibly at first, but it changes nonetheless. Former feelings of self effacement, feelings of dependence on the Absolute begin to lose meaning, and instead self glorification begins to assert itself. You begin to delight in the knowledge that you are indeed a self positing being!

I began to understand for the first time what was meant by the biblical teaching, "Blessed are the poor in spirit…," which means, blessed are those who do not feel that they are sufficient unto themselves; blessed are those who feel that of themselves they can do nothing.

The experience of that Sunday morning really jolted me to the core. It jolted me from the spiritual malaise into which I had fallen. I disappeared into an unoccupied room of the hotel, knelt down and said fervent prayers of thanksgiving. I had been preserved, and there was nothing to dissuade me from this conviction.

After about half an hour of silent prayer, I assembled the hotel staff in the small conference room of the hotel, which, fortunately, had been left intact, and together we tried to establish the source of the explosion. We were not using gas for the kitchen that particular weekend as the cylinders had no gas. Whenever the cylinders were empty we had to have them refilled in Dar es Salaam. We used charcoal that weekend; so the idea of a gas cylinder having exploded did not arise. Had it been just a fire breaking out, we might have suspected one of the employees or one of the hotel guests having carelessly thrown a burning cigarette butt somewhere in the hotel. But now the explosion! What caused such a big explosion? Could it have been a case of sabotage by any of the guests from the mining villages of Mpepo, Lukalasi, and now Mbaha and Mkili? These people could have had access to dynamite which was used for blasting rocks at the mines. There was a remote possibility of that kind of thing happening. But why would one do that? In any case, the explosion occurred in the north wing of the hotel which is normally inaccessible to hotel guests. Could one have done that out of mere spite?

I asked each one of the employees to say exactly where he was at the time of the explosion, and it turned out that beside myself, the most fortunate person that morning had been Mama Mihanjo. She was one of the hotel cleaners, and normally at the time the big explosion occurred she would have been cleaning my suite. Infact she had been to the suite only seven minutes before the explosion, but as she put it, "I left my brushes and washing powders in the toilet of the suite and went out of the hotel briefly to buy fish which some boys were selling. Just as I was buying the fish, there was this deafening sound of the explosion. Only seven minutes or so had separated me from death!"

We were all amazed and everybody shook hands with Mama Mihanjo and said *pole* to her. But we had drawn a blank as far as the cause of the explosion was concerned. I only hoped that someday this mysterious explosion would be explained.

As I was leaving the conference room I met a group of white tourists in the hotel lobby, which was still intact, fortunately. All of them had their luggage with them, and they were checking out of the hotel. They looked scared and angry.

An elderly gentleman who appeared to be German by nationality judging from his heavy English accent and pronunciation approached me and asked, "You are the owner of the hotel?"

"Yes," I answered.

"Ja, Ja, and how do you expect visitors to stay in a hotel where you allow bombs to explode?" He asked.

"Was it a bomb which caused the explosion?" I asked.

"So you cannot tell the sound of an exploding bomb?"

"No sir, I have no experience of these things."

"Have there been any casualties?"

"None that I know of, so far."

"Thank God for that. Had the bomb exploded on that side of the hotel, many people would have died. You see, I spent thirty years in the army, and I can assure you that the bomb which exploded here was pretty powerful," said the elderly gentleman.

"But who could have planted a bomb here? We do not know about these things here. We hear about the IRA bombing buildings in London, or of bombs exploding in the Gaza strip, but here such things have never happened," I remarked.

"All the same, you must be vigilant. I would advise you to take strict security measures here. Anybody coming to the island must be thoroughly searched," said the elderly gentleman.

"Where do you go from here, Sir?" I asked.

"Dar es Salaam. I'm going to stay in Dar es Salaam for a week before I fly home to Frankfurt, Germany. It's a pity we have to cut short our stay here. It is a very nice place, this. But our safety must take priority, you know?"

"Of course. Where in Dar are you going to stay? I was going to suggest we meet in Dar and talk some more about how best we can ensure the safety of our guests here. You seem to be a man of experience in these things."

"Before we came this way we stayed at Mikocheni Hotel in Dar. In fact our trip here was arranged by Mikocheni Hotel."

"I should have known that; but my colleague didn't tell me that your group was from Mikocheni. You see, both this and Mikocheni hotels are under the same management. I suggest then that you check in at Mikocheni, and I will meet you there tomorrow evening. I will ring Mikocheni and make reservations for you. If you leave now and spend the night at Iringa, you should be in Dar by evening tomorrow. I will drive to Mbambabay later this morning and ring Dar from there. Our telephone line was disrupted by the blast, you know. Tomorrow morning I will drive to Songea and catch the ATC flight in the afternoon. Let's meet tomorrow evening then."

"Alright. By the way, would it be possible for you to bring a list of the names of all the guests who slept here during the past week, and their addresses, of course? We will do some investigation."

"Thanks. I will do that," I said. "So long, until we meet again in Dar."

* * * * *

Mr. Rebman, the German tourist who had arrived from our hotel on Ngindo Island, was listening to *Taarab* near the swimming pool of Mikocheni Hotel. He and several other tourists were captivated by the soft voice of Khadija from Zanzibar. Other guests were carousing in the main bar of the hotel and our hotel bar attendants were busy serving the customers. Among the attendants were Vicky Mango and Renofrida Msola. These two, although looking like bar maids and serving the customers in the bar, were in fact, highly trained security officers. Both of them were high school graduates with several months of overseas training in security matters.

As I was crossing the bar I saw Vicky sitting on the laps of a white man whom I had seen at Ngindo the previous week. I was positive that I had seen the man at Ngindo; and in fact, the man had left the island hotel at around 10.00 am the previous Friday, in the company of other guests. The man was busy fondling Vicky, and Vicky seemed to be responding favourably.

After I had spotted Mr. Rebmann I approached him and exchanged a few words with him. I suggested to him that when he felt he has had enough of *Taarab*, we might meet in the hotel lobby from where I would take him to a private room for a chat. He agreed to accompany me right away; and in a few minutes we ensconced ourselves in my private office room.

"Now my friend," said the elderly German guest, "let us try to pull our heads together about the mystery of the bomb. By the way, has this matter been reported in the press or announced on the radio?"

"No, not at all. I rang my partner, Tom, from Mbambabay yesterday and informed him about the explosion, but we both agreed not to have the matter publicized as yet. I also asked the police at Mbambabay not to have the matter publicized. I feared that if sabotage was involved, and if the culprit was one of the foreign tourists, publicizing of the news would be the surest way of hastening his exit from the country."

"That was very wise of you," said Mr. Rebman. "Whoever did it, seeing that not a word has been said about it, will think that the explosion has probably been attributed to gas or something else. So he won't leave in undue haste, in case he is a foreigner."

Mr. Rebman stopped for a moment to take a pinch of snuff. Then he looked at me and asked, "Now, where do we begin? Did you remember to bring the list of names as I suggested?"

"Yes, what I did was to bring the actual registration cards for the last two weeks."

I took a large brown envelope in which I had stuffed the registration cards filled by guests as they checked in at Ngindo hotel during the last two weeks.

Mr. Rebmann was more than pleased at my ingenuity. He said, "This is marvellous. You see, the way I look at the problem is this: a time bomb was used to blow up your hotel; and if that was the case, the person who put the bomb could not be among those who were at the hotel at the material time the bomb went off. It is unlikely that he would have stayed at a place where a bomb had been timed to explode. So you may as well eliminate those of us who left after the explosion yesterday. Bombs, you see, can be timed to explode after any length of time, but for fear of the bomb being discovered before it actually explodes, no sane person would time a bomb to explode after a week or a month, unless he was double sure that there was no possibility of it being discovered earlier. But also no sane person would wish his bomb to go off too soon after his departure from the scene for fear of being suspected. So, by a process of elimination we come to a time interval of twenty four to forty eight hours. Let us then sort out the guests who left the hotel on Friday and Saturday."

It was not difficult to do this sorting out, since Ngindo Hotel was only a modest thirty-room hotel and the number of guests who had actually slept in the hotel during the past two weeks did not exceed eighty. Those who had left between Friday and Saturday were twenty one. I remarked casually, " Mr. Rebmann, this is like looking for a needle in a hay stack."

"No, no, my friend," Mr. Rebmann objected. "Just be patient. Do as I have suggested. We may come up with something."

We had a stack of twenty one registration cards on the table, and we started scrutinizing them one by one: the names, the addressees of where they came from and where they were proceeding to; their nationalities, their passport numbers, and so on. A few had European names, but the majority had local names: Ndunguru, Mapunda, Mosha, Mkude, Simba and the like.

However, there were five names: two Asian and three European, which gave their nationalities as Pakistani, Indian, British, Italian, and French. They all had written that they would be proceeding back to Dar. Their passport numbers were clearly given.

"Where do we go from here, Mr. Rebmann?" I asked, feeling the futility of the exercise.

"Don't give up so easily. There could be something there."

At this juncture I remembered the white man I had seen fondling Vicky in the bar. I told Mr. Rebmann, "There's a chap who left Ngindo last Friday who is right here in the hotel. He and one of our girls are necking on a seat in the bar."

"Are you sure he was at Ngindo last Friday?" Mr. Rebman asked as if he felt we were getting somewhere.

"Yes, I'm sure he was."

"Now, my friend, you must proceed very cautiously. If he is the person we're after, and if he detects you are in any way interested in him, he will dissolve into thin air before you know where you are."

"I think I know what I'll do," I said. "I will tell one of our boys to go and call Vicky, and we can then do a thorough job of it."

I pressed a buzzer and in a few minutes Shahibu, one of the bar attendants walked in. I told him to go and tell Vicky to come to the office, without of course letting the guest know that it was I who was calling her. Mr. Rebmann also left my office to rejoin his friends in the garden near the swimming pool. We both felt it would not be wise to have Vicky talking in the presence of Mr. Rebmann.

Vicky excused herself and left the amorous young man, promising she would rejoin him in a minute. She took a roundabout way, but ended up in my office. She was all smiles when she greeted me.

"Hi boss," she said, "how did you like that?"

"That what?"

"Me being fondled by that white man."

"Which white man?"

"Come off it boss, I'm sure you saw us necking as you were walking through the bar. I saw your furtive glance."

"Clever girl. Yes, indeed I saw you, and you seemed to be enjoying yourself."

"Well, that's part of the game, you know. I would not mind him parting with a few of his dollars tonight."

"Be a good girl, Vicky. Don't ever fall victim to people you don't know. That man could be a thug. He could throttle you in bed. Girls have been known to be throttled to death through casual sex."

"Don't scare me, *Mzee*, I want those dollars!"

"What's more, there's no taking chances these days, Vicky. Remember also that there is no such a thing as safe sex; for whether your partner is the carrier of a deadly virus or not, the damage done to the soul is exactly the same."

"Don't worry about me, *Mzee*, I was only kidding. I know exactly what I'm doing. Nobody can fool me into doing that sort of thing. You know me."

"There's a good girl," I said. "Now Vicky, what I called you for is a different matter. You have heard about our hotel on Ngindo Island?"

"Yes, our boss, Mr. Nyirenda, informed us about it yesterday, but he said we should not let people know about it. Is the hotel badly damaged?"

"The whole north wing has been ripped off. I was very lucky, I had gone to church when the bomb went off."

"So it was a bomb? Who could have put it there?"

"That's precisely why I have called you here. We are trying to trace who might have done it. Now the man you are talking with, was at Ngindo Hotel last week. He left the hotel last Friday at around 10.00 a.m. Experts tell me that bombs can be timed to explode after any length of time: ten, twenty or more hours as the perpetrator of the crime may decide. Now, that bomb went off forty eight hours after this man and others checked out of the hotel. We are trying to follow, where possible, each one of the guests who left the hotel one or two days before the bomb went off. Not that we have any reason for suspecting this particular man, but we are, as it were, blindly trying to trace any of our guests. It so happens that I have seen this man here, and like any of the others, I would like to rule him out. To begin with, have you found out what his name is, and where he is from?"

"He said he is called Claus," Vicky answered. "But I didn't ask him about his nationality. Look, we can easily find that out. I know he is in room 75. I will simply ring reception and ask Anna to bring us the man's registration card and so we can see what he has written."

Vicky lifted the receiver of my telephone and spoke to Anna who was at the reception desk that evening.

In a minute, Anna knocked at the door of my office, handed over not one registration card but two, and withdrew. Both Vicky and I examined the two cards. One was the card the guest had filled in a week ago when he first checked in at Mikocheni Hotel, and the other was the one he filled in last Saturday on his arrival from Ngindo. Both of them bore the name of Claus Schuller, South African. The same passport number was given in both cards, and the latest card showed that the guest was to leave for Johannesburg the coming Wednesday.

Then we both examined the cards of the five guests who had returned to Dar from Ngindo which I had brought. None of the names read Claus Schuller. None of the guests was South African! That's to say, no Claus Schuller from South Africa had been to Ngindo Hotel! So we had drawn a blank. But Vicky's sharp eyes had noticed something. She exclaimed, "Boss, look at the handwriting on these three cards!"

She put the two cards filled by Claus Schuller from Johannesburg and the card filled at Ngindo by a certain Roland Brown who had written he was British, with a British Passport issued in London. The handwriting was identical.

It flashed into my mind like a flash of lightning that this was the work of Van Meer, Msokonde's friend who had visited Ngindo Hotel a month ago, and had taken numerous photographs of the hotel.

As my heart began to pound strongly in my breast, I said, "That's it, that's it!"

At the same time, however, I realized that we were partly to blame. In the management of the two hotels we had not worked out proper communication mechanisms between the two hotels. For instance, the names of guests staying at Mikocheni Hotel in Dar were not sent to Ngindo in a kind of manifest when they wanted to visit Ngindo and vice versa. We allowed guests to register themselves anew when they got to Ngindo or Mikocheni hotel. We had been ill advised by some consultant that to operate the way we did would ensure a measure of autonomy for each of the hotels. But this loophole only allowed crooks to register themselves with fictitious names.

Vicky asked, "What'd you mean by saying 'that's it"?

"I mean ' your boy-friend' could be the person we are looking for. Vicky, from this moment on, I want you to use all your skill and brains until we have netted this man. Now go back to him and do all you can to make him believe that you are all his, tonight. But make absolutely sure that he doesn't enter his room in the next two hours. You can, for instance, suggest to him that you both sit near the swimming pool and listen to taarab. Tell him that he can have his drinks outside there while listening to *Taarab*, or better still, you can suggest hiring a taxi and taking him to La Prima Night Club, in which case I will give you enough money for the entrance fee and drinks for both of you."

"The second alternative is better," Vicky said, smiling. "Give me enough dough, boss, so I can buy my son his uniform tomorrow."

We both laughed. I gave her enough money, patted her on the shoulder and said, "Good luck, Vicky."

"Thanks," she said as she pocketed the money. "Leave it to me, boss. We won't be back until around midnight. I will see to it. And when we get back, I will slip through his fingers like a catfish. I know how to do it."

16

Vicky left my office and returned to the bar in search of her 'lover'. I also left, and by a roundabout way found my way to the swimming pool where I knew I would find Mr. Rebmann listening to *Taarab*. I joined Mr. Rebmann and stayed with him for a while. Then I whispered to him that we return to the office once again, and he dutifully obliged. As we were crossing the hotel grounds I could see, afar off, Vicky holding Claus Schuller by the hand and leading him into one of the many taxis whose drivers were only too eager to render service to night revellers. I knew Vicky had acted promptly and decisively.

Back in the office, I explained everything to Mr. Rebmann, and he kept nodding while listening to me. Then he said, "This must be the man you are looking for."

"I think so too," I said. "The reason why I suggested sending this man away with Vicky is to enable us to search his room, and I should like to ask you to assist me in this. With your experience you might discover something which could give irrefutable proof of his involvement in this affair, if it came to a showdown in a court of law."

"But how do we get into his room, do you have a spare key? And are you sure the man is gone?" Mr. Rebmann asked.

"Oh, yes. My business partner Mr. Nyirenda and I do have a master key to all the doors in this hotel, including the cupboards. You see, in the past we have had thugs hiding illicit drugs like mandrax and heroin in our cupboards. On one occasion a suspected drug pusher was given chase by the police and as he had been staying at the hotel he disappeared with our keys which he had not left at the reception desk as he ought to have done. When the police traced him here, they broke the door and cupboard of the room in which the man had been staying, and sure enough, they found boxes of mandrax in the cupboard. This gave our hotel a bad name for a while. It was as if this hotel was a den of drug pushers. Since then we decided to keep two master keys; and once in a while we do secret inspection of the rooms, especially if we have funny looking characters staying at the hotel. As for the man, oh, yes, he's gone to a nightclub with one of our security girls. I saw them leave as we were coming this way."

"Well, in that case, let's not waste any more time. Let's go to his room."

We both left the office and moved to room 75. I produced the master key and opened the door. I used another key and opened the cupboard. I had a slight apprehension that we might see a complicated suitcase, which would have made opening difficult. If he had a Samsonite box it would have presented no problem since one Samsonite can be opened by the key of any other Samsonite. But what if he had some strange box made in South Africa? Because of the gravity of the matter I was determined to tear open anything we found there, come what may.

My apprehension was quite uncalled for. This chap had no more than a canvas rucksack or backpack as these bags are sometimes called which many a tourist normally carries. So we had no problem with our search.

Mr. Rebmann unzipped the various pockets of the rucksack and carefully removed the contents. Two passports were removed: one issued in Johannesburg and belonging to Claus Schuller, and the other a British passport issued in London and belonging to Roland Brown, but both bearing the photograph of the same person. Mr. Rebmann continued emptying the rucksack. He removed beautiful photographs of Ngindo Hotel, and close ups of the various wings of the hotel. He even removed hand drawn sketches of the layout of the hotel. Then he removed some wires, and finally he touched something which made him withdraw his hand as if it had been bitten by a snake.

"That's it," he said, looking at me. "There's another bomb in here. But of course it hasn't been timed yet. These are the wires used to detonate the bomb. He probably had two of them. The other one he used to blow your hotel, and this was a spare one. And look at the passports. Such people always carry passports of several nationalities, to hide their true identity," Mr. Rebmann said while returning the contents in the rucksack.

What puzzled me was how this chap could have entered Tanzania carrying two bombs in a back pack without their being detected by the customs officials, and how the airline he had used could have failed to detect two bombs hidden in a rucksack!

Mr. Rebmann asked, "So what do you do now, my friend?"

"The rest is easy," I said. "I will first ring my partner and appraise him of these developments. You see, my partner is indisposed today, that's why he didn't come to the hotel. After talking with him we will call the police, and they will lay an ambush right here in this room and apprehend him when he returns from his reveling."

I looked at Mr. Rebmann and said, "I thank you sincerely for your assistance. Without you we wouldn't have got so far; and now you'd better go and enjoy yourself."

I drove immediately to Mr. Nyirenda's house which was only a matter of five minutes drive. I told him everything that had transpired and he in turn rang Mr. Msangi, the Regional Police Commander for the Dar es Salaam cosmopolitan region, who was also a great friend of ours. It took Mr. Msangi only half an hour to arrive at Tom's house accompanied by two armed constables, but all dressed in civilian clothes.

After a brief discussion it was decided to call two bomb disposal experts from Lugalo, the army headquarters. They arrived after half an hour.

From Tom's house we drove to the hotel. It was now nearing 22 hours, and Vicky and her boy friend would be returning to the hotel within the next hour or two. I led the little party to room 75, and took Schuller's rucksack from the cupboard. Then I removed the contents of the rucksack and carefully laid them on the table.

"Hey, gentlemen, there's your baby," Mr. Msangi said, showing the two army men the bomb. "We asked you to come so you can handle that thing, and assure us that it is harmless." One of the experts from the army examined the cables laid on the table and nodded. "These are used for detonating the bomb. If they aren't connected to the bomb, it can't explode."

We all crowded round the table to look at the bomb. One of the army men said, "This is a very powerful bomb. If detonated it could blow off at least a quarter of this building. These bombs are of South African make. See that slot there?" He asked pointing to a slot on the bomb. "That's where the detonating wire is hooked. Then the other end of the wire is lit, and it begins to burn slowly towards the bomb. You see, these detonating wires are made of special alloys, and it may take any length of time for the wire to burn its way to the bomb. The length of time it takes for the wire to burn out and detonate the bomb depends upon the diameter and particular length of wire used." He went on; "Just inside that slot is a small vial containing a concentration of Trinitrotoluene or TNT as we call it. The moment the necessary amount of heat reaches this vial, the explosion occurs." We were horrified, to say the least.

The army man put the bomb back in the rucksack, and I put back the other things: the photographs, the wires, and the passports. As for the passports, I did a little trick. The owner had placed them in two separate pockets of the rucksack. So he must have known from which pocket to retrieve the South African passport, and from which the British one. I purposely put both passports in one pocket.

The two police constables were instructed to remain in the room and put off the lights. I locked the room, and the rest of us went to the swimming pool where Tom and I entertained our three guests. Of course, we all kept our eyes open and watched the main entrance to the hotel with more than usual interest.

At around 23 hours a taxi *bubu* stopped on the driveway just in front of the main entrance to the hotel. Out staggered a young whiteman, followed by Vicky. Then Vicky stopped outside the taxi *bubu*, rummaged through her handbag, got the taxi fare and paid the driver. As the backlights of the taxi *bubu* disappeared in the distance, I whispered to Mr. Msangi. "There they are, Vicky and her boy friend."

"Let's give them ten minutes, shall we?" Mr. Msangi suggested.

"Seven minutes," said Tom. "I want to see this man arrested, so I can go home and rest. I had an injection this evening and the Doctor said I must rest."

"How about us Mr. Msangi? Do you still need us?" One of the army men asked.

"No, I don't think so. If we need you later we will send for you. You can continue enjoying yourselves and if we don't meet again to night, I will give you a tinkle tomorrow."

Vicky was an extremely intelligent woman. I had no doubt that she was going to slip through the young man's fingers like a slippery fish just as she had said she would. In fact, this is what she told me the next morning: as soon as they reached the reception desk she asked Anna to give her the key to room 75. Then she held Bwana Schuller lovingly by the hand and led him to his room. But only a few paces from the door of room 75 she handed the key to Claus and said, "I'll be with you in a minute; just go on ahead. I want to check if Juma has locked the door to the telex room." So saying she had darted into the pantry nearby and locked the door.

The seven minutes suggested by Tom were up, and the RPC, Tom and myself left the garden. Of course, by now poor Claus Schuller was facing the music, and Vicky was on her way home!

When we entered room 75 Claus had his arms raised over his head and the two constables were standing on either side of him, their pistols pointing at him. The RPC showed Claus an identification card announcing his rank as the police Commander of the Cosmopolitan region of Dar es Salaam. Then without wasting time he bade me open the cupboard. I removed the rucksack and placed it on the table once more. It was the RPC who started the ball rolling.

He showed Claus the registration card he himself had filled when he checked in at the hotel.

"Recognize this?" the RPC asked, bringing the card close to Schuller's eyes.

"Yes, sir, my registration card."

"Are Claus Schuller your real names?"

"Yes, Sir."

"And your nationality?"

"South African, as you can read there, Sir."

"And now this. Do you recognize this?" Mr. Msangi showed him the other registration card Claus had filled at Ngindo hotel.

"Did you fill this card? Mr.Msangi asked.

"No, Sir."

"Did you visit Ngindo Hotel last week?"

Claus hesitated a bit and looked at me. He knew I had seen and talked with him at Ngindo.

"Yes, I did," he answered.

"When did you leave Ngindo Hotel?"

"Last Friday."

"Did you register yourself when you checked in at Ngindo?"

"Yeah, I did."

"By what name? Roland Brown, eh?"

There was silence.

"Is this your handwriting?" Msangi pressed on, showing him the card again. "See, you wrote here that you were Roland Brown, and British."

Again there was silence.

"Show me your passport." Mr. Msangi demanded.

Claus reached for his rucksack and dipped his hand in the pocket in which he probably used to keep his South African passport. To his amazement he could feel two booklets in the pocket. For a fraction of a second he hesitated. If he pulled out both booklets he would expose himself to ridicule. If he pulled out one of them at random, he might pull out the wrong one - the British one. They were all the same size, and with smooth covers.

"For heaven's sake, don't waste our time," the RPC thundered. "Show us your passport!"

Claus extracted one of the passports from the rucksack. It was the British one with the name of Roland Brown on it!

"So you are Roland Brown and not Claus Schuller?"

"I am Claus Schuller."

"How come your passport reads Roland Brown? Why did you have to use an assumed name? Would I be wrong in assuming that you were trying to disguise your true identity for a sinister motive?"

Claus could not answer this barrage of questions from Mr. Msangi.

"And now," continued the RPC, "will you empty your rucksack? I want everything in that rucksack laid on the table."

With trembling hands Claus removed everything he had in the rucksack: the photographs, the wires, his clothes, his tooth brush and dental cream, old magazines, and finally, the bomb, and laid them on the table.

"And now Mr. Schuller you tell us what those things are. Forget about your clothes and dental cream. I will lead you. First what buildings are those in your photographs?"

"Ngindo Hotel."

"Did you take those photographs?"

Claus hesitated, because he knew if he said yes, he would be asked to produce the camera he had used; and he had no camera.

"Well," he answered, "I got them from a friend who had actually taken the photographs."

"Who is he?"

"Mr. Van Meer of Johannesburg. He advised me to visit the beautiful hotel on Ngindo Island while I was in Tanzania, and gave me photographs of the hotel just so I could see how beautiful it is."

"So you could see all those close up? What for? You must be joking! Now tell us about these wires. What are they?"

"Well, wires, as you say."

"Don't try to be clever. Answer my question, what are these wires; what're they used for?"

Before Claus could say anything, the RPC continued, "And which factory in South Africa manufactures these bombs?"

Claus Schuller had no answer to give. It was obvious to me, having studied and taught psychology for many years, that although Claus was a highly skilled bomb expert, he was not what you might call an experienced and hardened criminal. It could as well be that this was his first mission to carry out a criminal act. Had he really been an experienced criminal, defensive mechanisms would have automatically been called into play. He would for instance, have easily denied knowing anything about those photographs, wires and the bomb. He would have insisted that those things had been planted into his rucksack to incriminate him, although, of course, he would have been hard put to it to explain the similarity of the handwriting of Roland Brown in the registration card at Ngindo, and that of Claus Schuller in the card at Mikocheni, and also to explain the coincidence of the name he had used at Ngindo and the one appearing on the British passport.

The RPC went on, "Do you know that part of Ngindo Hotel has been blown off by a bomb?"

"No, I don't," answered Claus Schuller.

"Of course you don't, how could you know when you had conveniently run away from the scene of your crime? I am telling you now that forty eight hours after you had left Ngindo Hotel, there was a mighty blast which not only rocked the whole island, but also blew off part of Ngindo Hotel. Our army experts have examined your wires and your bomb, and they have confirmed that this kind of bomb is powerful enough to cause the kind of damage you caused at Ngindo."

"Did anybody lose life in the blast?" Claus asked, looking clearly terrified by what he had done.

That question, and his facial expression alone confirmed my suspicion that this man was a novice at what he had done, and that the pangs of remorse were already gnawing inside him.

" How many people did you wish dead?" The RPC asked.

" I did not wish anybody dead, sir."

As far as the RPC was concerned he had fulfilled his duty. He snapped his fingers and one of the plain-clothes constables snapped handcuffs on Claus Schuller's hands, and led him away to the Central Police Station. The rucksack and its contents were whisked away by the other constable.

17

Claus Schuller had written his statement at the Central Police Station. It was not so much a statement as an outright confession of guilt. All the details were given: his education, his employment in a bomb manufacturing factory in South Africa; his meeting with Mr. Van Meer who had subsequently sent him on this terrorist mission with the promise of a handsome reward. Schuller's statement mentioned something about a certain Msokonde who had cooperated with Van Meer in hatching out the hideous plan to blow Ngindo hotel so that for the immediate future, at least, the island might be abandoned as a dangerous place, thus leaving room for land speculators to try and acquire it. Then Schuller's statement went on to give details of how the parts of the bomb had been air freighted to Msokonde.

He revealed then that the bombs had been air freighted in bits and pieces hidden very cleverly in the false bottoms of cartoons of 'educational materials' sent to Mr. Msokonde from Van Meer of Johannesburg, two weeks before Schuller's arrival in Tanzania. After his arrival, Schuller had made contact with Msokonde, retrieved the materials, and assembled the bombs.

Schuller's statement went on to describe in detail how the mission had actually been carried out at the hotel. The point was made that he planted the bomb somewhere in the north wing of the hotel because having carefully studied the hotel, he knew that the north wing was not likely to be occupied by people on a Sunday morning when the bomb would explode.

Tom and I were summoned to the Central Police Station to confer with the RPC the following morning. He gave us Claus Schuller's statement to read. We read and re-read it. Indeed it made gruesome reading. How, I asked myself, can a person from a foreign country be prepared to indiscriminately kill people in another country simply in order to possess a rocky island hardly three square kilometres? As for Schuller's admission that he chose to plant the bomb in the northern wing of the hotel because the wing was not likely to be occupied on a Sunday morning, I thought, if this thug had known that my executive suite was located precisely in that wing of the hotel, and that Mama Mihanjo had the duty of keeping the suite clean even on Sundays, he would not have dared make that irresponsible statement as a justification for planting the bomb where he planted it!

Mr. Msangi wanted to know from us how we wanted the matter to proceed. Should the case be taken to court as it was, or should it wait until investigations were complete? Both Tom and I were of the opinion that it would not be in the best interest of Tanzania and justice, for that matter, to take Claus Schuller alone to court and leave Van Meer and Msokonde thriving like the cypress trees of Lushoto! If anything could be done, these two had to be brought to book.

But bringing Van Meer to book would involve the protracted process of extradition. How could we get Van Meer extradited from South Africa to Tanzania? It is true that Tom and I could make ourselves heard in the corridors of power. We could easily seek an appointment with the Minister for Legal and Constitutional Affairs who was also one of my former students; we could arrange to meet the Minister for Foreign Affairs; we could, if it became necessary, seek audience with the President himself by using our friend Shedrick Yalomba. Indeed we could use the influence of our friend Martin Wickman, who as you may remember, had mining interests in South Africa.

But all these approaches would amount to the same thing - getting the South African Government to agree to extradite Van Meer to Tanzania and this was by no means going to be easy - especially if you bear in mind that matters of extradition are governed by international law. No, we would use none of these approaches. We would use a simpler, more mundane approach to get Van Meer back to Tanzania. In fact we would get him to come to Tanzania of his own volition. We would simply lure him to come.

News about the bomb blast at Ngindo had neither been leaked to the press nor broadcast by Radio Tanzania, thanks to the remoteness of Lake Nyasa from Dar es Salaam. Before I left Mbambabay on Monday, I had specifically asked the Officer Commanding the police post at Mbambabay not to relay information about the bomb blast to the RPC at Songea as I was going to see the RPC in person that very morning.

Tom, with whom I had communicated the previous Sunday had, in turn, informed only Mr. Msangi. But he had asked him not to leak the information to the press or the Radio. We didn't want whoever was the culprit to dissolve into thin air before we knew where we were, as Mr. Rebman had put it.

"So how d'you get Van Meer here?" Mr. Msangi asked, looking at Tom and myself.

A plan was forming in my mind, or as some people would say, an idea was being born in my mind. I said, "Look, why don't we try this: we make up a story to the effect that last Sunday one of our hotel workers at Ngindo carelessly left a burning Chinese Stove near the gas cylinder outside the hotel kitchen. A leaking gas tube carrying gas into the stoves in the kitchen caught fire, and this resulted in the big blast of the gas cylinder. It was fire caused by the burning gas which gutted the whole wing of the hotel. There were no casualties, but the amount of loss suffered by the hotel is such that the hotel management has decided to abandon the site and rebuild the hotel at Mkili which, though a rapidly growing mining town, has no hotel. Hoteliers interested in buying the property on Ngindo Island are being invited for negotiations with the management.

"Let us have that kind of information broadcast on Radio Tanzania, and let us have it published in the press. Meanwhile we get Claus Schuller to cooperate with us. We will tell him to write Van Meer a letter, or better still, we will draft the letter and let Claus sign it."

"Ok, let's try it and see if it works," said the RPC. Tom also concurred with the idea. But he added, looking at me, "You draft the letter and let us see it this evening." Then turning to Mr. Msangi, he said, "Hope you can come to the hotel this evening? How about six thirty?"

"Six thirty's alright with me," Mr. Msangi agreed.

Tom and I left the RPC's office and drove to Mikocheni hotel. I went straight to the office and started drafting the letter to van Meer. This is what I wrote:-

"Dear Mr. Van Meer,

I want to give you the following good news.

The mission has been accomplished beyond my wildest expectation. The bloody thing was blown off exactly forty eight hours after my departure. I used both toys to make sure that the whole structure was razed to the ground.

The fools here have said that the blast was caused by an exploding gas cylinder (see the enclosed newspaper cutting). I've never met greater simpletons in my life! They couldn't even tell the difference between the sound of an exploding gas cylinder and that of an exploding bomb! They have published this information in almost all their papers here; and they have had the information broadcast on their radio. Oh, the fools!

As you will see in the newspaper cutting, the management of the hotel is inviting interested hoteliers to buy the property which is really nothing but the rocky island itself. The present owners have decided to rebuild the hotel at another site on the mainland close to a newly opened gemstone mine.

I was able to make contact with Mr. Msokonde without difficulty soon after my arrival. I assembled the toys and successfully carried out the mission. After completing my mission I'm holed up in Msokonde's house. It was Mr. Msokonde who suggested I write to you asking you to come as soon as possible so you can conclude the agreement about buying the island. He says he knows the present Minister for Lands, Water and Minerals so well that he thinks there won't be any difficulty clinching the deal. As a matter of fact, as soon as the newspaper article appeared, he went to see the relevant Minister and the Minister is all too eager to conclude the deal with us.

Msokonde has told the present Minister that you had been interested in buying the island when he himself was Minister, but that his former Permanent Secretary used to stand in the way. Do you know what? The former Permanent Secretary referred to is in fact the present owner, of the blasted thing who is eager to sell it!

The most interesting point is that the Minister says he will make sure that the negotiation will not be between you and the present owner but between you and his Ministry. The Government will simply compensate the present owner for the few things left on the island: the garden, the sheds, the lanes and the remains of the former hotel, and the island will revert to government as government property. You see, the present owner has no land title for the island. It appears he built the hotel there on the strength of the claim that his great great grand father had once lived on that island. How preposterous! Presumably customary land law gives him some kind of entitlement to the island. But the Minister says that by invoking certain powers vested in him by law, he will revoke this man's claim to the island, and you will buy it from the government. In any case, the owner himself is eager to sell the island. He needs the money badly to revive his business.

Msokonde insists that you come without delay, lest some other buyer comes forward. Do please send me a fax message using the number below and inform me of your arrival. I'm eagerly waiting for you, so we can return home together.

Regards,
Claus Schuller."

The Fax number I had given was that of my office, of course, and so was the post office box number and the telephone number.

I also spent some time polishing the text of the press release we were going to publish in the press and send to Radio Tanzania. When I was satisfied that everything was alright, I had the two messages neatly typed by Theresa, the hotel secretary, who was a very competent and trustworthy girl.

At 6.30 p.m. sharp the RPC's car arrived at Mikocheni Hotel. The three of us disappeared into the office before any prying eyes could notice what was happening.

I promptly displayed the two messages to my colleagues. They scrutinized both messages and made a few minor changes and additions; but the gist of both messages remained basically the same.

Tom pointed out that for the plan to succeed, we had to be absolutely sure that Claus did not have access to a telephone, fax, telex or anything of the sort, lest he should privately communicate with Van Meer. His only communication with Van Meer should be the false message we had prepared.

The RPC had a quick drink of gin and tonic and left immediately carrying the letter for Van Meer. He went straight to the Central Police Station to get Claus Schuller to sign the letter and also to get Schuller give him Van Meer's fax and telephone numbers.

It was not difficult to get these numbers from Claus; for the RPC told him that if within the next three days there would be no response from Van Meer, then he would know that he Claus, had given him wrong numbers, and the consequences on his part would be grave indeed. The RPC pointed out to Claus that so far no physical pain had been inflicted on him. But if there was no response from Van Meer within three days, his boys would begin to torture him, and he would then not only scream in his mother tongue, but he would also curse the day he was born.

Claus supplied all the information: Van Meer's postal address, telephone, telex and fax numbers, and he obligingly signed the letter. After all, in his heart what Claus really thought was that it was only fair that the man who had hired him to commit this heinous crime should also be brought to justice. Why should he suffer alone?

Armed with the information he was after, the RPC hurried back to the hotel. Theresa, the hotel Secretary, typed the numbers at the head of the letter, and in a few minutes the message had been faxed to Mr. Van Meer. The result was O.K.

Meanwhile, Tom had gone to see the Editor of the Daily News. Using his great influence, the kind of influence you acquire when moving in certain circles of society, he convinced the Editor that it was absolutely vital for the good of Tanzania, that his news item should appear on the front page of the Daily News the following morning, and the Editor had duly obliged.

From the Daily News office, Tom had hurried to Radio Tanzania with a copy of the news item. He wanted the news broadcast at prime time, 7 a.m the following day, through the External Service, to make sure that it was heard and understood as far away as South Africa! Here at Radio Tanzania there was no need to use any extraordinary influence, for the Director of Radio Tanzania, Mr. Andrew Manyama, was in fact, Tom's roommate in Northcote Hall at Makerere College. Mr. Manyama not only agreed to have the news item broadcast as requested, but to do Tom a special favour, he undertook to read the news himself, even though he had not been scheduled to read news that morning!

At the crack of dawn Mr. Manyama was in the air. The full story of the fate of Ngindo Hotel was being carried by radio waves throughout the cosmos. If per chance Mr. Van Meer had tuned in to the External Service of Radio Tanzania he no doubt had heard a confirmation of the fax message sent to him by Claus Schuller the previous evening.

Theresa walked into my office at 2p.m Wednesday carrying several fax and telex messages. I was interested in the one meant for Claus Schuller and sent from Johannesburg by Mr. Van Meer. In his message, Van Meer said simply that he was overjoyed by the information he had received, and that he was making arrangements to travel to Dar the coming Saturday. He would be arriving aboard a South African Airways flight No.847. He said he was looking forward to seeing Claus and asked if he could be booked at the Dar Sheraton.

This was it! Our plan had worked, and we were about to land our big fish. As for netting Msokonde who must have been an accomplice, that would be easy enough.

I immediately rang Tom who was resting at home, and apprised him of the new development. He in turn, rang Mr. Msangi, and it was finally arranged that we meet at the hotel at 6.30p.m that evening.

At this secret meeting it was Mr. Msangi who stole the show. Having read Van Meer's message to Claus, he said, "I suggest you two take it easy. This is now our baby. Barring unforeseen circumstances which might prevent Van Meer from coming, I can assure you that if he sets foot on Tanzanian soil this Saturday, he will be in our hands."

The South African Airways Boeing, flight 847 landed at Dar es Salaam International Airport dead on time. It was 16.15 hours. Mr. Van Meer had traveled first class, and like other first class passengers he emerged from the front door of the aircraft and proceeded to the VIP lounge for arriving passengers. As he was walking across the tarmac he raised his eyes to see if Claus was on the waving Bay of the airport building waiting for him. Claus wasn't there. He proceeded to the VIP lounge, and as usual, he handed his passport to an Immigration Officer to have it stamped. He settled down in a comfortable sofa seat to await his suitcase.

The suitcase arrived, and without any fuss, a customs officer chalked it, and allowed Mr. Van Meer to leave. A porter was carrying the suite case in front of him; then from behind came the Immigration Officer who had just stamped Mr. Van Meer's passport. He lightly tapped Mr. Van Meer on the shoulder and asked, "Mr. Van Meer?"

"That's right," Mr. Van Meer answered.

"There's a gentleman by the name of Claus waiting for you in that room over there," said the Immigration officer pointing to a side room close to the VIP lounge. "You see, here people meeting VIPs have to wait in that ante-chamber, so we don't mix them up with the arriving passengers."

So saying, the Immigration officer, who in fact happened to be one of Mr. Msangi's men who had been instructed to assume the role of an Immigration officer that particular day, opened the door of the ante-chamber, and ordered the porter to put Mr. Van Meer's suit case in the side room.

On entering the side room Mr. Van Meer saw Claus Schuller sitting between two people who were, in fact, fully armed plain clothes policemen. The RPC who was in uniform stood up as soon as Mr. Van Meer had entered, and he showed the incoming visitor a card identifying himself as the Police Commander of the Cosmopolitan region of Dar es Salaam.

"You are under arrest, Mr. Van Meer," the RPC said curtly.

"How'd you mean, under arrest?" Mr. Van Meer asked in astonishment. "This can't be true. I come here as an innocent businessman specifically invited to do business here, and you arrest me! This must be a case of mistaken identity. I can't be the man you are after."

"You are the man we're after," said Mr. Msangi. "Let me tell you this, you have never been invited to Tanzania; you have been lured to come. We have tricked you into coming to answer criminal charges of terrorism. For your information, acts of terrorism are punishable by death in this country."

Mr. Van Meer looked at Claus Schuller, not believing what was happening. He shouted at Claus, "Why did you write me that letter Claus?"

"I was forced to sign that letter," Claus answered.

"Damn you! Why did you agree to sign it? See where this has landed me now?" Shouted Van Meer.

"So you would have wished me to face the death penalty alone?" Claus shouted back.

"You are the one who sent me on the mission. We must face the consequences together."

Van Meer and Schuller were led away by Mr. Msangi's boys, not of course to the Sheraton as Mr. Van Meer had planned, but to the Central Police Station.

* * * * *

Tom rang Mr. Msokonde from Mikocheni hotel late in the evening of the same day Van Meer was netted.

"Hallo," said Tom after Msokonde had answered the call, "we haven't seen each other for quite some time. I wanted to suggest that you come for a drink here at the hotel if you are free. There is something I'd like to discuss with you."

"I'm ready to come for a drink," Msokonde said. "But to discuss something? Who am I to be invited to discuss anything important these days? In politics, you see, when you pass your zenith, that's the end of you. Only a few people manage to make political come backs!"

"It's nothing to do with politics," Tom said. "You may have read in the papers about the fiasco of our hotel business on Ngindo Island. We are really seriously thinking of selling whatever was salvaged from the wreck, and call it quits."

"Ah, yes, of course I have read about it. What a pity to spend money and effort to build a beautiful thing, only to end up having it reduced to ashes!"

"It takes the courage of a lion to withstand this kind of calamity. I remembered the other day, that in those happy days we were together at the Ministry you once told me of a South African gentleman who was interested in buying Ngindo Island. Do you still remember?"

"Of course I still remember. But you did not give me proper advice at the time. Had you done so we might have sold the island to that Boer, and who knows if my life would not have been different today? You see, making hay while it shines may be an old adage, but I can assure you that it is still valid."

"Yes, I realize now that the adage is not only true, but extremely wise too. Do you think the Boer might still be interested? I'm prepared to sell him the island and the remaining property on it. You see, the reason why I was reluctant to have the island sold at that time was that I knew I could claim it as my own on the basis of customary land law. My great great grandfather used to live on that island with his many wives. As you know, I was able to claim and possess the island. But now everything's gone up in smoke."

"So what do you want me to do?" Mr. Msokonde asked.

"Would it be possible for you to come over to the hotel, so we can talk the matter over in greater detail? We can talk about how we're going to contact the Boer, and about the price tag for the island. Rest assured that whatever deal we strike, you will have your cake."

"Right, I will come over in ten minutes," Mr. Msokonde said. "That is, if my Landrover can start. If you don't see me within quarter of an hour, then please come and fetch me. It will mean that the old bastard is not starting."

"If that's the case, why don't you leave the old thing alone? I am sending Maulidi, our hotel driver, to fetch you. He will take you back afterwards."

"That's better. I will be waiting here, then."

Tom looked at Mr. Msangi and me and smiled as he was replacing the telephone receiver. The trap had worked. Within a few minutes Msokonde would be in the hands of the law. When Maulidi started the Toyota Land Cruiser, I thought of my old student, Peter Msokonde, and my heart bled for him.

On arrival back at the hotel, Maulidi escorted Mr. Msokonde straight into the hotel office as he had been instructed to do. Tom and I had left the office some minutes before Msokonde's arrival. We did not want to be witnesses to the ordeal that was to follow. Msokonde walked straight into the hands of the law enforcers, and came face to face with the RPC who was smartly dressed in uniform. Msokonde was bundled away to the Central Police Station where he would meet his long time friend and 'prospective buyer' of Ngindo Island.

* * * * *

The case was heard by the High Court of Tanzania. Van Meer had been charged for masterminding a criminal act of terrorism; Claus Schuller for actually carrying it out, and Msokonde for collaborating with foreigners to commit what presiding judge Kazimoto called "the most dastardly act of terrorism ever committed in the United Republic of Tanzania within living memory'. In the opinion of justice Kazimoto, Msokonde's role in the affair was just as serious as that of the other two. Msokonde who was not only an indigenous citizen of Tanzania, but also a former Minister, should have known better than to cooperate in a murderous act of such magnitude.

Before the trial began, Van Meer insisted on being allowed to engage a lawyer to defend the trio, and the judiciary of Tanzania being a civilized judiciary, granted his request. On the advice of Msokonde, Advocate Kapinga was hired to defend the three. Try as he could, Advocate Kapinga who, otherwise was one of the most brilliant advocates in Tanzania, could not make up a credible case for the defense, because Claus Schuller's statement had said it all.

There was also plenty of circumstantial evidence against the three accused persons. For instance, Tom testified about Msokonde's relationship with Van Meer, with regard to the latter's wish to buy Ngindo Island. This was corroborated by Mr. Oswald Mkangama who produced in court the compliment slip written by Msokonde to Tom asking for advice on the technicalities of selling an island, since he wanted to sell Ngindo island to a certain Van Meer of Johannesburg. I testified about seeing Van Meer taking photographs of Ngindo hotel in the company of Peter Msokonde, and of course, the photographs exhibited in court had been given to Claus Schuller by Van Meer, according to Schuller's statement. There was also clear evidence to show that Claus Schuller had been to Ngindo Island two days before the fateful day.

All these pieces of circumstantial evidence gave Mr. Kapinga no chance to save the skins of his clients. Mr. Kapinga did, however, try capitalize on certain technicalities of law, but he met with stiff objection by the learned judge. The jury also unanimously returned a verdict of 'guilty.'

In the end the trio was sentenced to life imprisonment, although acts of terrorism like this one were punishable by death. Justice Kazimoto, using his discretionary powers, reasoned that since, by lucky chance, no death had been caused by the bomb blast, he would exercise leniency by passing life sentences on the three culprits.

Two years after a joint venture agreement had been signed between the Tanzania Government and Wickman's Company, and while the notorious trio headed by Van Meer was serving the life sentence meted out by Judge Kazimoto, the face of Unyanja was changing fast. The old dirt road along the lakeshore had been upgraded into an all weather road, and so was the dirt road between Mbinga and Mkili. Feeder roads to the new mines had been constructed, and work on providing electricity and water to the mines was in full swing. The inhabitants of Unyanga were flocking to the new mines in search of employment as unskilled labourers. Shedrick Yalomba had also visited the new mines a number of times on the pretext that as Minister for Lands, Water and Minerals he was monitoring development of the mines. The truth however, was that he was looking ahead to the future election year;

for at the mines he would meet groups of workers and draw their attention to the development he had brought to Unyanja!

Meanwhile, the reconstruction of Ngindo Hotel had been completed and booming business had resumed. The ploy of building a new hotel at Mkili had been useful in that it had helped to convince Van Meer that Ngindo Island was being abandoned. I was once again shuttling between Dar and Ngindo, while Tom was mainly confined to Dar.

While life seemed to have returned to normal, I began to notice that Tom's health was failing. I had a secret fear that Tom might be having some serious malady. His heavy smoking gave me cause for worry, and in fact, I sometimes told him to try and cut down on his smoking.

My fears were soon to be proved true. Martha and I were relaxing in the sitting room of our Kimara house in the outskirts of Dar when the telephone rang. It was 7.30 p.m. I went to answer the call.

" Hallo, this is Susan. Tom is feeling unwell, and I'm alone in the house, I thought I'd ask you to come along and give me a hand."

"We will be with you as soon as possible," I said.

I looked at Martha and said, "Susan says Tom is unwell, and she is asking us to go and give her a hand."

"You told me the other day that you didn't think Tom looked well," Martha said. "You are right. I did say that. Of late, Tom has developed a very dry persistent cough. I fear this may have some connection with his heavy smoking. Let's go and see what help we can give."

Martha and I left immediately and drove straight to Tom's house. On entering the house, we met Susan waiting for us in the sitting room. From the siting room we could hear Tom coughing violently - a dry unproductive cough, the kind of cough that can make one feel exhausted.

Susan led us into the bedroom where we found Tom propped up on pillows and looking frail and emaciated. Martha and I sat down near the bed and consoled him with the usual pole. He looked at Susan and said, " You tell them everything. They are the closest friends I have on earth."

Susan started to sob into her handkerchief before she could tell us anything; and Martha, who had been Susan's godmother at her wedding hugged her and whispered into her ear words of encouragement. Susan then plucked up courage and began to speak. "I am sorry," she said, " I don't have the strength to withstand seeing Tom like this."

"What's the matter?" I asked. "You know, Susan, that Martha and I are here to do everything we can to help. So tell us everything, so we can know what needs to be done."

Susan said, "You see, Tom hasn't been feeling well for several months. Of late, however, his cough has worsened, and he is in torment most of the time, especially during the night. We decided to see Dr. Kayombo, and he carried out a number of tests on him. Only yesterday he gave us the bad news that Tom has developed lung cancer." Susan stopped, and started sobbing again.

I felt that this diagnosis must be correct, considering the amount of nicotine Tom must have inhaled in his life. But this was not time to cry over spilled milk. It wasn't time for me to say, "My friend, if only you had heeded my advice not to smoke too heavily!" To say that kind of thing would be like twisting a knife in a raw wound. I had to think of a different line of approach.

"Tom," I said, stroking his arm, "My wife and I have heard what Susan has said, and take it from me, we deeply sympathize with you. But I want to say right away that this does not mean the end of the world."

"That's precisely what it means for me, Chris." Tom insisted amid cough howls.

"No, it doesn't," I said firmly. "By the way, did the Doctor say if the malignancy has reached an advanced stage?"

Susan said, "He said only a small part of the right lung shows signs of malignancy. That's to say, the cancer is just starting."

"There you are," I said reassuringly. "I make no pretence to medical or surgical knowledge, but I am told by my medical colleagues that a person can live with half of his lungs removed. If this cancer is operable I don't see why the malignant part can't be removed. I must seek out Dr. Kayombo and find out what the next step should be. Speed is of the essence in such cases. The longer we wait the more chance we give to the cancer to spread."

"But Chris," Tom said, "they say that when cancer is tempered with through an operation it spreads to other places. It metastasizes, as they say."

"C'mmon, Tom, don't talk about things you don't know. The trouble with all of us, the so called educated people is that we are so good at imagining things. You get a rash on the skin and you imagine you've got AIDS, simply because you have read or heard that a skin rash is one of the symptoms of AIDS. No, Tom I'm going to do everything in my power to help you."

"What're you going to do?" Tom asked, still feeling incredulous and frightened.

"I will speak to Dr.Kayombo first," I said. I charged out of the room like a mad bull. The idea of losing Tom was beginning to weigh on me. I went to the sitting room where I knew the telephone was, and rang Dr. Kayombo who, like Msokonde, was also one of my former students, in his case, at Kigonsera Secondary School. After I had made contact with him, we talked in low voices about Tom's chances. He told me that at the present stage of Tom's malignancy it was possible to cut off the affected portion of the lung, and Tom could live to see his great grand children. But Kayombo insisted that speed was absolutely necessary in dealing with this kind of situation. If anything was to be done, it had to be within the next two weeks. He said that the progression of these kinds of malignancies could sometimes be so fast that within a few weeks we might find out we have missed the boat. Dr. Kayombo said further that he was prepared to talk to his medical colleagues to see if the operation could be performed the following week.

However, I told him to hold on until I had consulted Tom on that point for, the point is really that I was thinking of having Tom treated overseas. Not that I had any doubt about the competence of the local doctors, but because I'd heard many specialist doctors complain about lack of the sophisticated equipment they needed. Add to that the fact that there were frequent power and water interruptions in Dar at the time. I could not countenance the possibility of power failing while Tom was on the operating table with his chest surgically opened!

I returned to Tom's bedroom wearing a broad smile. I sat on Tom's bed and said, "Kayombo says that at the present stage of the malignancy an operation to remove the affected part is possible, and if that could be done within the next week or two, you could live to see your great grand children."

Tom grinned when he heard this. I could see a glimmer of hope showing in his eyes. Martha and Susan embraced one another. I continued, "Tom, I want to ensure that you get the best treatment medical science can offer. We must get you to the best hospital we can find. I intend to ring Mr. Wickman of Lulea, Sweden, or better still, Linda Wickman and see what arrangements can be made. I will do that at the hotel to-night; and I will let you know the outcome of the conversation as soon as possible thereafter."

Tom said, "If you do contact Linda or her father, tell them we can pay for our passages to and from any place they suggest. The important thing is for them to help identify for us the best hospital I can go to, and of course, make the necessary booking for admission."

"Thanks Tom," I said. "I'll tell them that I will also seek Dr. Kayombo's opinion. I'm sure he can advise us on the best hospital for this kind of ailment. Our local doctors here have been referring patients to overseas hospitals for years. They must know which hospitals are good and which aren't."

I stopped for a while and then said, "In the meantime, Tom; I'm going to start a novena on your behalf, and I hope you will cooperate with me."

"What's a novena, Chris?" Tom asked.

"Well, it's a devotion or prayer said on nine consecutive days asking for some special blessing. In this case we will ask the good Lord to restore you to full health."

"Yes, Chris, the books you lent me have truly enlightened me on the meaning of prayer, and I now do believe in the efficacy of prayer. When you talked about these things in Diplomat Hotel, Stockholm that day, I was skeptical, to be frank. But after reading your books and trying to put into practice some of the things written in those books, I have had real surprises. I do not mean, of course, that whatever I have asked for has been granted; for as almost all your books emphasize, prayer does not mean making small speeches to God telling him what he should do for you. Prayer should not always be petitioning the Almighty for something. Other kinds of prayer: adoration, praise, thanksgiving, reparation, and above all, contemplation are just as important, if not more so. I tell you Chris, the peace or tranquility of mind; the joy I have sometimes experienced when I tried to pray as your books urge, is beyond description in words."

I was astounded to hear this little sermon coming from Tom who, only a few years ago asked me in Diplomat Hotel, stockholm. "What is it that prayer does? Do prayers influence God's decisions?" As I sat there on the side of the bed looking at Tom's frail body I could not help thinking that Tom's point of conversion or encounter with God, like that of St. Paul on the road to Damascus, must have occurred sometime in the past few years. Inwardly, I felt a secret joy to think that the few books I had lent him could have been instrumental in bringing about this spiritual encounter between him and his Lord.

"Tom," I said, "I am glad you found those books helpful. Now while I go and set our plans in motion, I wish to commend you to the Lord. Have full confidence and unwavering faith in his healing power."

I left Martha with the Nyirendas so she could help Susan in case there was an emergency. I drove to Mikocheni Hotel where we had excellent communication facilities.

It took me two hours of waiting to get in contact with Linda Wickman by phone. I slowly explained to her Tom's problem, and emphasized the point that we wanted to take Tom to the best hospital which she and her father would recommend. Linda said she would talk the matter over with her father and she would revert to me by faxed message the following morning.

At nine the following morning, Theresa walked into my office carrying a bunch of papers. I quickly identified the faxed message from Lulea Sweden. In the message, Martin Wickman had not only said he sympathized with the turn of events, but he had also said he had contacted the most famous oncologist in Germany, a certain Professor Gotlieb, owner of a clinic in Cologne. The Professor had agreed to have Tom admitted in his clinic as soon as he could be flown there. The message went on to say that Linda would be at Frankfurt Airport to meet Tom, if we could let them know of Tom's travel arrangements.

That morning was quite hectic for me. I first drove to Tom's house to communicate to the family Wickman's reply as contained in the faxed message. We then agreed that I should contact Dr. Kayombo for the necessary referral documents. This we did by phone, and the doctor agreed to have the documents ready for collection in the afternoon of the same day. Then I visited the bank, the Bureau de change, the German Embassy, and the offices of Lufthansa, in that order. By mid - morning of the third day everything was set for Tom and Susan to travel to Frankfurt and on to Cologne. It was then that I sent a faxed message to Linda Wickman informing her of Tom's arrival at Frankfurt airport in two days' time.

Tom's illness was a guarded secret among his family, my family and Dr. Kayombo. Our hotel employees had no idea what was happening, not even Vicky who was normally very smart in reading the 'signs of the times'! The only person who might have guessed that something was in the offing could have been Theresa, who might have read the faxed message from Lulea. So I called her to the office and told her that Tom was going for medical check-up in Europe, but that we didn't want people to know. I warned her against saying anything about it to anybody. I said, If I hear anything resembling the information in the faxed message you brought me the other day, you lose your job, understand?"

"Believe me, boss, I did not even read the message," Theresa said. "Even if I had read it, I wouldn't dare divulge it to anybody. That's what I was vetted for, and I've worked here ever since this hotel started. No such thing has happened to me."

"There's a good girl", I said "Keep it up. Learn to keep certain things to yourself."

* * * * *

When the Lufthansa jet took off from Dar es Salaam International Airport, there were only Dr. Kayombo, Martha and myself to wave Mr and Mrs. Nyirenda goodbye.

The Nyirendas were met by Linda Wickman at Frankfurt International Airport. From there they travelled by train to Cologne. After Tom's admission in Professor Gotlieb's clinic, a number of tests were carried out to confirm Dr. Kayombo's diagnosis as recorded in the letter of referral from Dar es Salaam.

When Susan Nyirenda rang me from Cologne, she informed me that Tom's operation had been performed successfully the previous day. I realized that it was the day I ended my novena. I was overwhelmed with joy.

Susan continued to reveal that Tom had come round after the anaesthetic, but that he was fitted with all kinds of tubes, and was in the intensive care unit. Everybody at the clinic was, however, assuring her that the operation had gone beautifully and that there was no cause for worry. I urged Susan to keep relaying to me these medical bulletins on Tom at least for the next couple of days until she was satisfied that Tom was out of danger.

True to her promise, she rang me every evening for the next four days, until finally she said that Tom had been moved from the ICU to an ordinary ward, and that the tubes that had sustained his life during the past few days had now been removed.

Two weeks passed, and there was no communication between me and Susan. In the third week, Susan rang to say that the doctors had said they would be discharging Tom in a week's time. She said also that it had been arranged with Linda Wickman that after Tom's discharge, he should go to Sweden for two months convalescence. So we were not to expect the Nyirendas for the next two months.

* * * * *

Tom Nyirenda and his wife Susan arrived at Dar es Salaam Airport on a Sunday afternoon. The same little group of friends: Dr. Kayombo, Martha and myself, was at the airport to meet them. As Martha embraced Susan and I embraced Tom, I could hardly restrain tears of joy. Here was Tom looking as virile as he was when we were students at Makerere College. Here was a person who had been preserved or spared from almost certain death.

As we were driving home from the airport, I got lost in thought. Life of the recent past presented itself before my mind's eye like images on a cinema screen. Tom had been spared from the clutches of terrorists out in the outskirts of Lulea. I had been spared from the telescopic rifles of the same terrorists in the wilderness of Abisko National Park. Only recently, I had been spared miraculously from a bomb blast, and now Tom had been spared from a deadly disease, albeit a self-induced one. What did all this mean? I could find no answer other than that supplied by the Psalmist, "*The Lord shall preserve thy going out and coming in from this time forth and even for evermore*". Indeed Tom and I had been spared.

This book has been approved to be used as an O level set book for Tanzania's Secondary Schools. It is also a great novel to be read for personal entertainment as well as to enrich your grasp of the english language.

For other exciting books visit our website at www.mkukinanyota.com

UNITED REPUBLIC OF TANZANIA

MINISTRY OF EDUCATION AND VOCATIONAL TRAINING

Certificate of Approval

NO. 778

Title of Publication: Spared

Author: S. N. Ndunguru

Publisher: Mkuki na Nyota Publishers Ltd.

ISBN: 9987 417 04 3

This book was approved by EMAC on 8 *(date)* 1 *(month)* 2007 *(year) to be a* Reader *for Form* 3 & 4 *in* ***Secondary Schools*** *in Tanzania as per* 2005 *Syllabus.*

R. A. Mpama
CHAIRPERSON
EMAC

SEAL

Printed in the United States
By Bookmasters